THE STOLEN PARTY

An anthology of women's stories

THE STOLEN PARTY

An anthology of women's stories compiled by Veronica Green

Published by the Press Syndicate of the University of Cambridge
The Pitt Building, Trumpington Street, Cambridge CB2 1RP
40 West 20th Street, New York, NY 10011–4211, USA
10 Stamford Road, Oakleigh, Melbourne 3166, Australia

First published 1993

Printed in Great Britain at the University Press, Cambridge

A catalogue record for this book is available from the British Library

ISBN 0 521 44806 9 paperback

Cover illustration by Rosemary Woods

GO

Contents

	page
Introduction	7
Dual Control *Elizabeth Walter*	9
Smoke *Ila Mehta*	19
The Stolen Party *Liliana Heker*	26
The Earth *Djuna Barnes*	32
Looking for a Rain God *Bessie Head*	40
A Visit from the Footbinder *Emily Prager*	44
The Kiss *Angela Carter*	71
To Hell with Dying *Alice Walker*	75
Here We Are *Dorothy Parker*	82
Two Hanged Women *Henry Handel Richardson*	91
The Lottery *Marjorie Barnard*	96
Daughter *Anne McCaffrey*	103
Notes on the writers and their stories	123
Acknowledgements	135

Introduction

Why a collection of *short* stories? Surely 'real' stories are more interesting or useful? Not necessarily so. This collection offers readers the chance to meet a wider range of good writers and so extend their literary horizon. It would take a lot longer to meet such a range of writers if we had to read a full-length novel by each one.

These stories were chosen because they are an enjoyable read. That does not mean that the reader can relax into a pleasurable fantasy world. The stories are directly relevant to the lives of each of us and explore different kinds of close relationships. Sometimes it is the closest of family relationships – father, mother, brother, husband or wife – or it may be that the relationship skips a generation, or perhaps there is an exploration of friendship. Each of these stories will merit close attention, and they offer the chance for discussion of students' own relationships. To read 'Daughter', for example, without allowing for a recollection of one's own family stories would be a sadly wasted opportunity. (In the notes at the back of the book there is an indication of how long each story might take to read aloud.)

Short stories have a basic appeal and are the form of story that we all hear as small children. All the nursery tales were short stories. It is only later as adults that we enjoy long tales. Nevertheless, there always remains a place for the short story since it carries within its structure all the most important characteristics of story telling in a condensed form. The short story has its own genre, quite separate from poetry, drama and novel. I hope this selection will show that.

Veronica Green

Dual Control

Elizabeth Walter

'You ought to have stopped.'

'For God's sake, shut up, Freda.'

'Well, you should have. You ought to have made sure she was all right.'

'Of course she's all right.'

'How do you know? You didn't stop to find out, did you?'

'Do you want me to go back? We're late enough as it is, thanks to your fooling about getting ready, but I don't suppose the Bradys'll notice if we're late. I don't suppose they'll notice if we never turn up, though after the way you angled for that invitation . . .'

'That's right, blame it all on me. We could have left half an hour ago if you hadn't been late home from the office.'

'How often do I have to tell you that business isn't a matter of nine to five?'

'No, it's a matter of the Bradys, isn't it? You were keen enough we should get asked. Where were you anyway? Drinking with the boys? Or smooching with some floozie?'

'Please yourself. Either could be correct.'

'If you weren't driving, I'd hit you.'

'Try something unconventional for a change.'

'Why don't you try remembering I'm your wife –'

'Give me a chance to forget it!'

'– and that we're going to a party where you'll be expected to behave.'

'I'll behave all right.'

'To me as well as to other women.'

'You mean you'll let me off the leash?'

'Oh, you don't give a damn about *my* feelings!'

'Look, if it hadn't been for you, I should have stopped tonight.'

'Yes, you'd have given a pretty girl a lift if you'd been on your own. I believe you. The trouble is, she thought you were going to stop.'

'So I was. Then I saw she was very pretty, and – Christ, Freda, you know what you're like. I've only got to be polite to a woman who's younger and prettier than you are – and believe me, there are plenty of them – and you stage one of your scenes.'

'I certainly try to head off the worst of the scandals. Really, Eric, do you think people don't know?'

'If they do, do you think they don't understand why I do it? They've only got to look at you . . . That's right, cry and ruin that fancy make-up. All this because I *didn't* give a pretty girl a lift.'

'But she signalled. You slowed down. She thought you were going to . . .'

'She won't jump to conclusions next time.'

'She may not jump at all. Eric, I think we ought to forget the Bradys. I think we ought to go back.'

'To find Cinderella has been given a lift by Prince Charming and been spirited away to the ball?'

'She was obviously going to a party. Suppose it's to the Bradys' and she's there?'

'Don't worry, she couldn't have seen what we looked like.'

'Could she remember the car?'

'No, she didn't have time.'

'You mean she didn't have time before you hit her.'

'God damn it, Freda, what do you expect me to do when a girl steps in front of the car just as I decide – for your sake – I'm not stopping? It wasn't much more than a shove.'

'It knocked her over.'

'She was off balance. It wouldn't have taken more than a touch.'

'But she fell. I saw her go backwards. And I'm sure there was blood on her head.'

'On a dark road the light's deceptive. You saw a shadow.'

'I wish to God I thought it was.'

'Look here, Freda, pull yourself together. I'm sorry about it, of course, but it would make everything worse to go back and apologise.'

'Then what are you stopping for?'

'So that you can put your face to rights and I can make sure the car isn't damaged.'

'If it is, I suppose you'll go back.'

'You underestimate me, as usual. No, if it is I shall drive gently into that tree. It will give us an excuse for arriving late at the Bradys' and explain the damage away.'

'But the girl may be lying there injured.'

'The road isn't that lonely, you know, and her car had obviously broken down. There'll be plenty of people willing to help a damsel in distress . . . Yes, it's as I thought. The car isn't even scratched. I thought we might have a dent in the wing, but it seems luck is on our side. So now, Freda, old girl, I'll have a nip from that flask you've got in your handbag.'

'I don't know what you mean.'

'Oh yes you do. You're never without it, and it needs a refill pretty often by now.'

'I can't think what's come over you, Eric.'

'Call it delayed shock. Are you going to give it to me or do I have to help myself?'

'I can't imagine – Eric, let go! You're hurting!'

'The truth does hurt at times. Do you think I didn't know you had what's called a drinking problem? You needn't pretend with me.'

'It's my money. I can spend it how I choose.'

'Of course, my love. Don't stop reminding me that I'm your pensioner, but thanks anyway for your booze.'

'I didn't mean that. Oh Eric, I get so lonely, you don't know. And even when you're home you don't take any notice of me. I can't bear it. I love you so.'

'Surely you can't have reached the maudlin stage already? What are the Bradys going to think?'

'I don't give a damn about the Bradys. I keep thinking about that girl.'

'Well, I give a damn about the Bradys. They could be important to me. And I'm not going to ruin a good contact because my wife develops sudden scruples.'

'Won't it ruin it if they know you left a girl for dead by the roadside?'

'Maybe, but they won't know.'

'They will. If you don't go back, I'll tell them.'

'That sounds very much like blackmail, and that's a game that two can play.'

'What do you mean?'

'Who was driving the car, Freda?'

'You were.'

'Can you prove that?'

'As much as you can prove that I was.'

'Ah, but it's not as simple as that. Such an accusation would oblige me to tell the police about your drinking. A lot of unpleasant things would come out. I should think manslaughter is the least you'd get away with, and that could get you five years. Because please note that apart from that swig I am stone cold sober, whereas your blood alcohol is perpetually high. In addition, you're in a state of hysteria. Who d'you think would be believed – you or I?'

'You wouldn't do that, Eric. Not to your wife. Not to me.'

'Sooner than I would to anyone, but it won't come to that, will it, my dear?'

'I've a good mind to –'

'Quite, but I should forget it.'

'Eric, don't you love me at all?'

'For God's sake, Freda, not that now, of all times. I married you, didn't I? Ten years ago you were a good-looking thirty –'

'And you were a smart young salesman on the make.'

'So?'

'You needed capital to start your own business.'

'You offered to lend it me. And I've paid you interest.'

'And borrowed more capital.'

'It's a matter of safeguarding what we've got.'

'What we've got. That's rich! You hadn't a penny. Eric, don't start the car like that. You may not be drunk but anyone would think you are, the way you're driving. No wonder you hit that girl. And it wasn't just a shove. I think you've killed her.'

'For God's sake, Freda, shut up!'

'Well, it was a good party, wasn't it?'

'Yes.'

'Moira Brady's a marvellous hostess.'

'Yes.'

'Jack Brady's a lucky man. We ought to ask them back some time, don't you think?'

'Yes.'

'What's got into you? Cat got your tongue? You're a fine companion. We go to a terrific party and all you can say is Yes.'

'I'm thinking about that girl.'

'She was all right, wasn't she? Except for some mud on her dress. Did she say anything about it?'

'She said she'd fallen over.'

'She was speaking the literal truth. Now I hope you're satisfied I didn't hurt her.'

'She certainly looked all right.'

'You can say that again. Life and soul of the party, and obviously popular.'

'You spent enough time with her.'

'Here we go again. Do you have to spend the whole evening watching me?'

'I didn't, but every time I looked, you were with her.'

'She seemed to enjoy my company. Some women do, you know.'

'Don't torment me, Eric. I've got a headache.'

'So have I, as a matter of fact. Shall I open a window?'

'If it isn't too draughty . . . What was the girl's name?'

'Gisela.'

'It suits her, doesn't it? How did she get to the Bradys'?'

'I didn't ask.'

'It's funny, but I never saw her go.'

'I did. She left early because she said something about her car having engine trouble. I suppose someone was giving her a lift.'

'I wonder if her car's still there?'

'It won't be. She'll have got some garage to tow it away.'

'Don't be too sure. They're not so keen on coming out at nights in the country, unless something's blocking the road.'

'I believe you're right. That's it, isn't it – drawn up on the grass verge.'

'Yes. And Eric, that's her. She's hailing us.'

'And this time, I'm really going to stop.'

'What on earth can have happened?'

'It looks like another accident. That's fresh mud on her dress.'

'And fresh blood on her head! Eric, her face is all bloody!'

'It can't be as bad as it looks. She's not unconscious. A little blood can go a very long way. Just keep calm, Freda, and maybe that flask of yours will come in handy. I'll get out and see what's up . . . It's all right, Gisela. You'll be all right. It's me, Eric Andrews. We met at the Bradys' just now. My dear girl, you're in a state. What in God's name happened? Has someone tried to murder you? Here, lean on me . . .'

'Eric, what's the matter? Why have you left her alone? Gisela . . .'

'Christ, Freda, shut that window! And make sure your door's locked.'

'What is it? You look as if you'd seen a ghost.'

'She *is* a ghost . . . Give me that flask . . . That's better.'

'What do you mean – a ghost?'

'There's nothing there when you go up to her. Only a coldness in the air.'

'But that's nonsense. You can't see through her. Look, she's still standing there. She's flesh and blood – blood certainly.'

'Is there blood on my hand?'

'No, but it's shaking.'

'You bet it is. So am I. I tell you, Freda, I put out my hand to touch her – I *did* touch her – at least, I touched where she was standing – but she's got no body to touch.'

'She had a body at the Bradys'.'

'I wonder.'

'Well, you should know. You hung round her all the evening, making a spectacle of yourself.'

'I never touched her.'

'I'll bet it wasn't for want of trying.'

'Now I think of it, nobody touched her. She always seemed to stand a little apart.'

'But she ate and drank.'

'She didn't eat. She said she wasn't hungry. I don't remember seeing a glass in her hand.'

'Rubbish, Eric. I don't believe you. For some reason you don't want to help her. Are you afraid she'll recognise the car?'

'She has recognised it. That's why she's here. We – we must have killed her on the way to the party that time when we nearly stopped.'

'You mean when *you* nearly stopped. When you hit her. Oh God, what are we going to do?'

'Drive on, I think. She can't hurt us.'

'But she could get inside the car.'

'Not if we keep the doors locked.'

'Do you think locked doors can keep her out? Oh God, I wish I'd never come with you. Oh God, get me out of this. I never did anything. I wasn't driving. Oh God, I'm not responsible for what he does.'

'Oh no, you're not responsible for anything, are you, Freda? Does it occur to you that if it hadn't been for your damned jealousy I should have stopped?'

'You've given me cause enough for jealousy since we were married.'

'A man's got to get it somewhere, hasn't he? And you were pretty useless – admit it. You couldn't even produce a child.'

'You're heartless – heartless.'

'And you're spineless. A sponge, that's all you are.'

'I need a drink to keep me going, living with a bastard like you.'

'So we have to wait while you tank up and make ourselves late for the Bradys'. Do you realise, if we'd been earlier we shouldn't have seen that girl?'

'It's my fault again, is it?'

'Every bloody thing's your fault. I could have built up the business a whole lot faster if you'd put yourself out to entertain a bit. If I'd had a wife like Moira Brady, things would be very different from what they are.'

'You mean you'd make money instead of losing it.'

'What do you mean – losing it?'

'I can read a balance sheet, you know. Well, you're not getting any more of my money. "Safeguarding our interests" I don't think! Paying your creditors is more like it.'

'Now look here, Freda, I've had enough of this.'

'So have I. But I'm not walking home so there's no point in stopping.'

'Then try getting this straight for a change –'

'Eric, there's that girl again.'

'What are you talking about? Anyone would think you'd got DTs.'

'Look – she's bending down to speak to you. She's trying to open your door.'

'Christ!'

'Eric, don't start the car like that. Don't drive so furiously. What are you trying to do?'

'I'm trying to outdistance her.'

'But the speed limit . . .'

'Damn the speed limit! What's the good of having a powerful car if you don't use it? . . . That's right. You hit the bottle again.'

'But the way you're driving! You ignored a halt sign. That lorry driver had to cram on his brakes.'

'What the hell! Look round and see if you can see her.'

'She's right behind us, Eric.'

'What, in her car?'

'No, she seems to be floating a little way above the ground. But she's moving fast. I can see her hair streaming out behind her.'

'Well, we're doing seventy-five ourselves.'

'But we can't go on like this for ever. Sooner or later we've got to get out.'

'Sooner or later she's got to get tired of this caper.'

'Where are we? This isn't the way home.'

'Do you want her following us home? I want to lose her. What do you take me for?'

'A bastard who's ruined my life and ended that poor girl's.'

'No one warned me you'd ruin mine. I wish they had. I might have listened. Warnings are only given to the deaf . . . Look again to see if Gisela's still following.'

'She's just behind us. Oh Eric, her eyes are wide and staring. She looks horribly, horribly dead. Do you suppose she'll ever stop following us? Gisela. It's a form of Giselle. Perhaps she's like the girl in the ballet and condemned to drive motorists to death instead of dancers.'

'Your cultural pretensions are impressive. Is your geography as good?'

'What do you mean?'

'I mean where the hell are we? I swear I've never seen this

road before. It doesn't look like a road in southern England. More like the North Yorkshire moors, except that even there there's some habitation. Besides, we couldn't have driven that far.'

'There's a signpost at this next crossroads if you'll slow down enough for me to read . . .'

'Well?'

'I don't understand it, Eric. All four arms of the signpost are blank.'

'Vandals painted them out.'

'Vandals! In this desolate, isolated spot? Oh Eric, I don't like this. Suppose we're condemned to go on driving for ever?'

'No, Freda, the petrol would give out.'

'But the gauge has been at nought for ages. Hadn't you noticed?'

'What? So it is. But the car's going like a bird.'

'Couldn't you slow down a bit? I know you didn't for the signpost, but she – she's not so close behind us now . . . Please, Eric, my head's still aching.'

'What do you think I'm trying to do?'

'But we're doing eighty . . . I knew it. We'll have to go on driving till we die.'

'Don't be such an utter bloody fool. I admit we've seen a ghost – something I never believed existed. I admit I've lost control of this damn car and I don't know how she keeps running on no petrol. I also admit I don't know where we are. But for all this there's got to be a rational explanation. Some time-switch in our minds. Some change of state.'

'That's it! Eric, what's the last landmark you can remember?'

'That blanked-out signpost.'

'Not that. I mean the last normal sign.'

'You said there was a halt sign, but I must say I never saw it.'

'You drove right through it, that's why. We shot straight in front of a lorry. I think – oh Eric, I think we're dead.'

'Dead! You must be joking. Better have another drink.'

'I can't. The flask's empty. Besides, the dead don't drink. Or eat. They're like Gisela. You can't touch them. There's nothing there.'

'Where's Gisela now?'

'A long, long way behind us. After all, she's had her revenge.'

'You're hysterical, Freda. You're raving.'

'What do you expect but weeping and wailing? We're in Hell.'

'The religious beliefs of childhood reasserting themselves.'

'Well, what do you think Hell is? Don't hurry, you've got eternity to answer in. But I know what *I* think it is. It's the two of us driving on alone. For ever. Just the two of us, Eric. For evermore.'

Smoke

Ila Mehta

Ba comes back this evening by the five o'clock train. Shubha glanced at her watch. It was only four o'clock, still some time to go. A vast sea of overpowering emptiness engulfed her being. Nothing left to do. Nothing . . . except wait.

Her hands wandered over the books lying on the table and picked one up. It was a fat book written in English, on women's health problems and their treatment. It opened with the picture of a naked woman, bared in vivid detail, sketched with dexterity. For clinical purposes only, of course!

She slammed it shut, pushed it back and walked out of the room on to the open balcony. She stood still. The oppressive tormenting afternoon was still astride the earth, its heat permeating every nook and cranny. 'Like my own emptiness,' she thought. 'Not a hollow neutral vacuum but this leaden emptiness, opaque and solid.'

'The russet evening shall wax but a few moments only. And then all will be dark again.' A wan smile on her lips. Shubha stepped back into the room.

Just half-past four. Driving her car towards the station, Dr Shubha scolded herself, 'You're becoming neurotic, Shubha. The sun itself looks like a dark blot to you.'

Suddenly her belly tightened. Was everything ship-shape for Ba's homecoming? All details seen to? Like unwinding the reel of a film, she went over the house slowly, room by room, in her mind's eye. Nothing amiss. All in order. Each corner had been cleaned with care. But suppose . . . ? Well – her practice and the clinic really left her with no time to spare. Her mother-in-law knew it well. And those few snatched private moments, well, forget it. It's just as well Ba did not get to know.

Swiftly, suddenly, a cold shiver rose from the pit of her stomach to her throat, with a chilling reminder – the picture! The photograph of Subodh had been left undusted, with the dirty grey string of dried flowers hanging around it. She had forgotten to place a fresh wreath. And with it remained Bapuji's photograph too. Ba would of course go straight up to them, first thing on coming home.

Framed in dry dead petals, Subodh's face smiled unmoving in black and white – like the printed picture of Krishna on last year's Diwali card, chucked on top of a heap of discarded papers.

Shubha gripped the steering wheel hard.

The ashtray beside the telephone – had it been cleaned? Often, ever so often, in these past few days she had sat there smoking as she talked over the telephone. Suppose Ba were to ask why we needed an ashtray at all in our house? What then? Oh God! There was no time now to turn back to the house. She parked the car and went into the station.

The train arrived on time. The luggage was stacked into the car. Shubha slid behind the wheel and started the engine and Ba got in beside her. Inching her way through milling crowds, sounding the horn intermittently, slamming the brakes on at traffic lights, she drove homeward. The driving, the traffic and the tortuous progress, she had grown used to it all now and could manage mechanically.

Ba talked. As she talked, the fatigue of the journey was shot through with the lively satisfaction that lit her face. Crisply, rapidly, Ba went about recounting the little happenings and family gossip, as she always did. Like the clickety-clack of needles knitting all the inconsequential details into the common tale of the extended Indian family. Aunt, nephew, cousin, grandmother, criss-crossing relatives gathered together to celebrate or to mourn.

The car ran on. For it had to run on. Ba's words flitted out of the window like dry leaves swept along by the afternoon breeze. Shubha was quiet. Her thoughts hovered round that ashtray near the telephone – cigarette ash wafting in the air.

Home at last. Pressing the horn twice to summon a servant, Shubha ran up the stairs, not even waiting for Ba to alight. She went straight to the telephone. No ashtray there.

Damn it! She herself had put it away into the cupboard this morning.

Ba came up and headed straight for the photographs. Bapuji and Subodh smiled through the film of dust. Only four months after Shubha had stepped in as a bride, father and son had died together in a road accident.

A crystal bowl decked with fresh young blossoms had dashed to the floor and shattered. Since then, like the myriad splinters of glass, were the moments of life, each to be picked up, one at a time, and one by one to be put away.

Ba carefully cleaned the photographs, knelt down and touched her head to the floor. Rising she turned to Shubha, and on a faintly reproachful note asked, 'My dear, how did so much dust gather? Surely you remembered the fresh flowers and obeisance every day?'

One could make excuses – of a patient being ill, of visits to be paid. But words failed Shubha. She walked out of the room slowly.

Outside, she stood leaning against the rails of the balcony. Ba, she thought, must now be busy washing and bathing. At once she was seized with an irrepressible urge. The small space between thumb and finger throbbed palpably.

She went back to the room. Ba would take a long time in her bath. She pulled the packet out with an impatient hand and lit a cigarette, taking in the first few drags hungrily. Oh God. Just to quell the restless thirst of hours . . .

One cigarette smoked, she lit another from its end. This too must be finished before Ba came out. She stood there and inhaled the smoke, deep and steady.

But how long can this go on? How long can the act be kept secret from her mother-in-law? There was the clinic, of course, where she could smoke. But Ba might just walk in there too, one day.

The sound of the bathroom door being unlatched broke her reverie. She flung the cigarette away, turned her head and peered. No, Ba was not yet back. She drew a long breath and sank down on the cane sofa.

Life. How it stretched, interminably. How inexorably the seconds tick away. No might in the world can give them a shove and push them back. Time . . .

A wave of exhaustion swept over her all at once. As if she had been plodding miles, carrying a heavy load. Now she only wanted to sit, just sit with a cigarette dangling from her listless hand.

'Don't you have to go to the clinic today?' Ba's voice reached out to her.

'I'm going,' she answered and snapped her purse shut. But she remained rooted to the sofa. The prospect of the clinic was depressing.

The faces that waited for her there would be dismal, every one of them, some bereft of all hope. To think of them was to enter that grey realm. 'I cannot eat a morsel, doctor.' 'A fever of 100° since yesterday.' 'The swellings on the feet have not gone down.' Some throats riddled with swollen glands, some tumours destined to live or to die, a ceaseless tug-of-war and unending complaints.

She heaved a sigh and just as she was about to rise and leave, Ba came in. Seeing Shubha still sitting, she drew up the cane chair opposite and sat down.

'Shubha, the wedding was really great fun, very enjoyable. Oh dear, we – now let's see, how many years since I last saw a wedding? Your wedding, of course, and after that – oh well. But Mama was hurt that you did not attend. I explained to him of course. She is a doctor, I said. She has a commitment to her patients. Far be it from me to come in the way of her duty. What do you say? Isn't that so?'

An answer. One must say something now. Ba was waiting for a response. That is how it should be – some give and take, some conversation. Without these mundane exchanges, a home would freeze into one of those two-dimensional stills. Her voice, pitched a shade too high, broke the lengthening pause. 'How did Indu look as a bride? Was she dressed heavily for the occasion?'

'Yes indeed, dear. They had called in one of these make-up artistes, you know. A full hundred rupees she charged! But Indu looked like a doll.'

Ba pulled herself up a bit and continued, 'You know Shubha, it really makes me laugh. These modern girls are all just dolls, mere dolls. Not a jot of idealism, noble thoughts or sensibilities.'

Shubha gazed out in silence as the evening spread its shadow over the earth. She looked into the falling darkness.

'Come, now. You'll be late for work,' Ba said.

She rose to her feet. Clutching the balustrade firmly in hand, she walked down the steps and out of the house. She started the car but after a moment switched off the engine. She would walk to the clinic today, she decided. It was a short distance only and she was in no mood to drive.

At the clinic, she found a large number of patients waiting for her. She took them all in at a glance. At the end of the line sat a man, neatly dressed, middle-aged. Their eyes met. An enigmatic smile played on his lips as he said, 'Have been waiting for you for ever so long.'

Shubha reacted with a start. It was not the words or voice so much, but the smile that was disquieting. A shiver of fear. As if this man could read her mind, as if he knew all, inside out.

She turned her eyes away in haste. She sat erect in her chair and answered, a trifle too loudly, a trifle too crisply. 'Sorry, I have been delayed a bit.'

One after another the patients came up to her. Some were advised to consult a specialist – for some an X-ray, for others merely an aspirin. It was all so routine. And the eyes of the man at the end of the queue somehow radiated strength to her – enhancing her capabilities, her insight, and her confidence. Yet there was that undercurrent of irritability, a weariness, an overwhelming desire just to let go . . . !

She glanced at him. His smile hurt her, chased her about like some little whirligig, a sparkler that children light on festival nights which scatters a shower of thrill and fear round and round in its zig-zag trail.

Most of the patients had departed. It was his turn now – the last one. A cigarette. The urgent need to smoke welled up in her. Her fingers pulled out a cigarette from her purse. The man sprang up and lit it with his own lighter.

'Thank you.'

Then he sat down in the chair opposite her.

'Latika has been unwell since yesterday. Doctor, would you please come?'

His voice now struck dread, like his haunting smile. His

words, so mildly spoken, were a confident invitation. Beneath the words lay the phrases unspoken: 'I know . . . I know it all . . . everything.'

She stood up and said, 'Yes, let's go. We shall watch for a day or two and then maybe call in a specialist.'

He picked up Shubha's black bag, walked ahead to his car and held the door open for her. A moment's pause, then Shubha got into the front seat. He closed the door with care, walked round and got in beside her, behind the wheel.

Latika was of course not yet as well as she ought to be, but even so her condition did not quite merit a house call. Still, Shubha spent a long evening at their house. Long-ailing spinster and her bachelor brother together managed to keep the evening scintillating. She sat for a long time with the brother and sister, savouring the easy flow of conversation. The simple chatter that bounces off the walls of a house giving it the dimensions of a home. The fear of that smile had now vanished. Skeins of laughter and companionship spun a shimmering cocoon around her.

'Doctor, stay back and eat with us,' begged Latika. Shubha sprang up with a start and looked at her watch. Nine-thirty! Ba waited at home for her. She had returned . . .

'No thank you – it's late. Some other time.' She stood up.

'I had no idea of your taste in these things. I have a number of imported brands – cigarettes as well as drinks,' he said.

'Oh, no! It's only occasional . . .' Murmuring, she crossed to the telephone, called the clinic, told the compounder to close for the day. She felt agitated, scared. She had lingered too long – the laughter, the jokes – for no good reason on earth. Life. She felt alive, and yet dreaded the very touch of life, afraid to come alive.

He drove her home in his car. Lifting her black bag in his hand, he offered to carry it upstairs. But she took it from him with a 'No, thank you.'

He did not move but looked at her and said softly, 'Will you not come again, unless my sister is ill? Won't you come over just to see us? We have really enjoyed your visit. You see, we are quite alone.'

She could no longer stand there. Mumbling a formal 'Yes, of course' she quickly climbed the steps.

A cloud of sweet incense hit her at the door. She entered

the living room and saw the two photographs of Subodh and Bapuji draped with thick garlands of flowers. A bunch of incense sticks burned before them. The air hung heavy with the sweet scent. Ba sat on the floor facing the pictures, reciting the Gita.

Softly, Subha crossed over to her room, put down her purse and taking the cigarette packet out, tucked it away into the cupboard. She washed her hands and face and rinsed her mouth with antiseptic. When she returned to the living room Ba had finished her recitation and was spooning the food onto the plates.

'I had to call on a patient. It got late,' she said and sat down to eat.

Ba's hand stopped still in mid-air. Shubha jumped up and prostrated herself before Subodh's photograph. Subodh was smiling at her – a distant lifeless smile framed by fresh voluptuous blossoms.

As they ate, Ba began to talk again. Shubha barely heard her. Her thoughts, her being were still in Latika's house. The faint whiff of aftershave lotion, light laughter. 'You see, we are quite alone.' His words, his eyes . . .

'We are quite alone.' She heard the words distinctly again and looked up, startled. It was Ba talking to her.

'I told your Mama, "Do not worry for us, brother, what if we are quite alone? I and my dear Shubha, we are quite apart from others."'

Shubha looked down at her plate as she ate. Ba spoke on.

'Mama was all too full of praise, dear. "Shubha is indeed a saint," he said. "Her life is like an incense stick. It burns itself to release its fragrance into the world."'

Suddenly, Ba's voice ceased. Shubha looked up at her mother-in-law. A deep frown knitting her brow, Ba stared steadily into the corner opposite. She got up and walked over, and picked up something from the floor.

'Shubha, what is this?' Ba's voice cracked. Like hard dry earth. The barren sunbaked earth cracks, willy-nilly, along deep jagged fissures.

With thin trembling fingers Ba held up the burnt-out stub of a cigarette.

Translated from the original Gujarati by Sima Sharma

The Stolen Party

Liliana Heker

As soon as she arrived she went straight to the kitchen to see if the monkey was there. It was: what a relief! She wouldn't have liked to admit that her mother had been right. *Monkeys at a birthday?* her mother had sneered. *Get away with you, believing any nonsense you're told!* She was cross, but not because of the monkey, the girl thought; it's just because of the party.

'I don't like you going,' she told her. 'It's a rich people's party.'

'Rich people go to Heaven too,' said the girl, who studied religion at school.

'Get away with Heaven,' said the mother. 'The problem with you, young lady, is that you like to fart higher than your ass.'

The girl didn't approve of the way her mother spoke. She was barely nine, and one of the best in her class.

'I'm going because I've been invited,' she said. 'And I've been invited because Luciana is my friend. So there.'

'Ah yes, your friend,' her mother grumbled. She paused. 'Listen, Rosaura,' she said at last. 'That one's not your friend. You know what you are to them? The maid's daughter, that's what.'

Rosaura blinked hard: she wasn't going to cry. Then she yelled: 'Shut up! You know nothing about being friends!'

Every afternoon she used to go to Luciana's house and they would both finish their homework while Rosaura's mother did the cleaning. They had their tea in the kitchen and they told each other secrets. Rosaura loved everything in the big house, and she also loved the people who lived there.

'I'm going because it will be the most lovely party in the whole world, Luciana told me it would. There will be a magician, and he will bring a monkey and everything.'

The mother swung around to take a good look at her child, and pompously put her hands on her hips.

'Monkeys at a birthday?' she said. 'Get away with you, believing any nonsense you're told!'

Rosaura was deeply offended. She thought it unfair of her mother to accuse other people of being liars simply because they were rich. Rosaura too wanted to be rich, of course. If one day she managed to live in a beautiful palace, would her mother stop loving her? She felt very sad. She wanted to go to that party more than anything else in the world.

'I'll die if I don't go,' she whispered, almost without moving her lips.

And she wasn't sure whether she had been heard, but on the morning of the party she discovered that her mother had starched her Christmas dress. And in the afternoon, after washing her hair, her mother rinsed it in apple vinegar so that it would be all nice and shiny. Before going out, Rosaura admired herself in the mirror, with her white dress and glossy hair, and thought she looked terribly pretty.

Señora Ines also seemed to notice. As soon as she saw her, she said:

'How lovely you look today, Rosaura.'

Rosaura gave her starched skirt a slight toss with her hands and walked into the party with a firm step. She said hello to Luciana and asked about the monkey. Luciana put on a secretive look and whispered into Rosaura's ear: 'He's in the kitchen. But don't tell anyone, because it's a surprise.'

Rosaura wanted to make sure. Carefully she entered the kitchen and there she saw it: deep in thought, inside its cage. It looked so funny that the girl stood there for a while, watching it, and later, every so often, she would slip out of the party unseen and go and admire it. Rosaura was the only one allowed into the kitchen. Señora Ines had said: 'You yes, but not the others, they're much too boisterous, they might break something.' Rosaura had never broken anything. She even managed the jug of orange juice, carrying it from the kitchen into the dining-room. She held it carefully and didn't spill a single drop. And Señora Ines had said: 'Are you sure you can manage a jug as big as that?' Of course she could manage. She wasn't a butterfingers, like the others. Like that blonde girl with the bow in her hair. As soon as she saw Rosaura, the girl with the bow had said:

'And you? Who are you?'

'I'm a friend of Luciana,' said Rosaura.

'No,' said the girl with the bow, 'you are not a friend of Luciana because I'm her cousin and I know all her friends. And I don't know you.'

'So what,' said Rosaura. 'I come here every afternoon with my mother and we do our homework together.'

'You and your mother do your homework together?' asked the girl, laughing.

'I and Luciana do our homework together,' said Rosaura, very seriously.

The girl with the bow shrugged her shoulders.

'That's not being friends,' she said. 'Do you go to school together?'

'No.'

'So where do you know her from?' said the girl, getting impatient.

Rosaura remembered her mother's words perfectly. She took a deep breath.

'I'm the daughter of the employee,' she said.

Her mother had said very clearly: 'If someone asks, you say you're the daughter of the employee; that's all.' She also told her to add: 'And proud of it.' But Rosaura thought that never in her life would she dare say something of the sort.

'What employee?' said the girl with the bow. 'Employee in a shop?'

'No,' said Rosaura angrily. 'My mother doesn't sell anything in any shop, so there.'

'So how come she's an employee?' said the girl with the bow.

Just then Señora Ines arrived saying *shh shh*, and asked Rosaura if she wouldn't mind helping serve out the hot-dogs, as she knew the house so much better than the others.

'See?' said Rosaura to the girl with the bow, and when no one was looking she kicked her in the shin.

Apart from the girl with the bow, all the others were delightful. The one she liked best was Luciana, with her golden birthday crown; and then the boys. Rosaura won the sack race, and nobody managed to catch her when they played tag. When they split into two teams to play charades, all the boys wanted her for their side. Rosaura felt she had never been so happy in all her life.

But the best was still to come. The best came after Luciana blew out the candles. First the cake. Señora Ines had asked her to help pass the cake around, and Rosaura had enjoyed the task immensely, because everyone called out to her, shouting 'Me, me!' Rosaura remembered a story in which there was a queen who had the power of life or death over her subjects. She had always loved that, having the power of life or death. To Luciana and the boys she gave the largest pieces, and to the girl with the bow she gave a slice so thin one could see through it.

After the cake came the magician, tall and bony, with a fine red cape. A true magician: he could untie handkerchiefs by blowing on them and make a chain with links that had no openings. He could guess what cards were pulled out from a pack, and the monkey was his assistant. He called the monkey 'partner'. 'Let's see here, partner,' he would say, 'Turn over a card.' And, 'Don't run away, partner: time to work now.'

The final trick was wonderful. One of the children had to hold the monkey in his arms and the magician said he would make him disappear.

'What, the boy?' they all shouted.

'No, the monkey!' shouted back the magician.

Rosaura thought that this was truly the most amusing party in the whole world.

The magician asked a small fat boy to come and help, but the small fat boy got frightened almost at once and dropped the monkey on the floor. The magician picked him up carefully, whispered something in his ear, and the monkey nodded almost as if he understood.

'You mustn't be so unmanly, my friend,' the magician said to the fat boy.

'What's unmanly?' said the fat boy.

The magician turned around as if to look for spies.

'A sissy,' said the magician. 'Go sit down.'

Then he stared at all the faces, one by one. Rosaura felt her heart tremble.

'You, with the Spanish eyes,' said the magician. And everyone saw that he was pointing at her.

She wasn't afraid. Neither holding the monkey, nor

when the magician made him vanish; not even when, at the end, the magician flung his red cape over Rosaura's head and uttered a few magic words . . . and the monkey reappeared, chattering happily, in her arms. The children clapped furiously. And before Rosaura returned to her seat, the magician said:

'Thank you very much, my little countess.'

She was so pleased with the compliment that a while later, when her mother came to fetch her, that was the first thing she told her.

'I helped the magician and he said to me, "Thank you very much, my little countess."'

It was strange because up to then Rosaura had thought that she was angry with her mother. All along Rosaura had imagined that she would say to her: 'See that the monkey wasn't a lie?' But instead she was so thrilled that she told her mother all about the wonderful magician.

Her mother tapped her on the head and said: 'So now we're a countess!'

But one could see that she was beaming.

And now they both stood in the entrance, because a moment ago Señora Ines, smiling, had said: 'Please wait here a second.'

Her mother suddenly seemed worried.

'What is it?' she asked Rosaura.

'What is what?' said Rosaura. 'It's nothing; she just wants to get the presents for those who are leaving, see?'

She pointed at the fat boy and at a girl with pigtails who were also waiting there, next to their mothers. And she explained about the presents. She knew, because she had been watching those who left before her. When one of the girls was about to leave, Señora Ines would give her a bracelet. When a boy left, Señora Ines gave him a yo-yo. Rosaura preferred the yo-yo because it sparkled, but she didn't mention that to her mother. Her mother might have said: 'So why don't you ask for one, you blockhead?' That's what her mother was like. Rosaura didn't feel like explaining that she'd be horribly ashamed to be the odd one out. Instead she said:

'I was the best-behaved at the party.'

And she said no more because Señora Ines came out into the hall with two bags, one pink and one blue.

First she went up to the fat boy, gave him a yo-yo out of the blue bag, and the fat boy left with his mother. Then she went up to the girl and gave her a bracelet out of the pink bag, and the girl with the pigtails left as well.

Finally she came up to Rosaura and her mother. She had a big smile on her face and Rosaura liked that. Señora Ines looked down at her, then looked up at her mother, and then said something that made Rosaura proud:

'What a marvellous daughter you have, Herminia.'

For an instant, Rosaura thought that she'd give her two presents: the bracelet and the yo-yo. Señora Ines bent down as if about to look for something. Rosaura also leaned forward, stretching out her arm. But she never completed the movement.

Señora Ines didn't look in the pink bag. Nor did she look in the blue bag. Instead she rummaged in her purse. In her hand appeared two bills.

'You really and truly earned this,' she said handing them over. 'Thank you for all your help, my pet.'

Rosaura felt her arms stiffen, stick close to her body, and then she noticed her mother's hand on her shoulder. Instinctively she pressed herself against her mother's body. That was all. Except her eyes. Rosaura's eyes had a cold, clear look that fixed itself on Señora Ines's face.

Señora Ines, motionless, stood there with her hand outstretched. As if she didn't dare draw it back. As if the slightest change might shatter an infinitely delicate balance.

Translated by Alberto Manguel

The Earth

Djuna Barnes

Una and Lena were like two fine horses, horses one sees in the early dawn eating slowly, swaying from side to side, horses that plough, never in a hurry, but always accomplishing something. They were Polish women who worked a farm day in and day out, saying little, thinking little, feeling little, with eyes devoid of everything save a crafty sparkle which now and then was quite noticeable in Una, the elder. Lena dreamed more, if one can call the silences of an animal dreams. For hours she would look off into the skyline, her hairless lids fixed, a strange metallic quality in the irises themselves. She had such pale eyebrows that they were scarcely visible, and this, coupled with her wide-eyed silences, gave her a half-mad expression. Her heavy peasant face was fringed by a bang of red hair like a woolen tablespread, a color at once strange and attractive, an obstinate color, a color that seemed to make Lena feel something alien and bad-tempered had settled over her forehead; for, from time to time, she would wrinkle up her heavy white skin and shake her head.

Una never showed her hair. A figured handkerchief always covered it, though it was pretty enough, of that sullen blonde type that one sees on the heads of children who run in the sun.

Originally the farm had been their father's. When he died he left it to them in a strange manner. He feared separation or quarrel in the family, and therefore had bequeathed every other foot to Una, beginning with the first foot at the fence, and every other foot to Lena, beginning with the second. So the two girls ploughed and furrowed and transplanted and garnered a rich harvest each year, neither disputing her inheritance. They worked silently side by side, uncomplaining. Neither do orchards complain when their branches flower and fruit and become heavy. Neither does the earth complain when wounded with the plough, healing up to give birth to flowers and to vegetables.

After long months of saving, they had built a house, into which they moved their furniture and an uncle, Karl, who had gone mad while gathering the hay.

They did not evince surprise nor show regret. Madness to us means reversion; to such people as Una and Lena it meant progression. Now their uncle had entered into a land beyond them, the land of fancy. For fifty years he had been as they were, silent, hard-working, unimaginative. Then all of a sudden, like a scholar passing his degree, he had gone up into another form, where he spoke of things that only people who have renounced the soil speak of – strange, fanciful, unimportant things, things to stand in awe of, because they discuss neither profits nor loss.

When Karl would strike suddenly into his moaning, they would listen awhile in the field as dogs listen to a familiar cry, and presently Lena would move off to rub him down in the same hard-palmed way she would press the long bag that held the grapes in preserving time.

Una had gone to school just long enough to learn to spell her name with difficulty and to add. Lena had somehow escaped. She neither wrote her name nor figured; she was content that Una could do 'the business'. She did not see that with addition comes the knowledge that two and two make four and that four are better than two. That she would some day be the victim of knavery, treachery or deceit never entered her head. For her, it was quite settled that here they would live and here they would die. There was a family graveyard on the land where two generations had been buried. And here Una supposed she, too, would rest when her wick no longer answered to the oil.

The land was hers and Una's. What they made of it was shared, what they lost was shared, and what they took to themselves out of it was shared also. When the pickle season went well and none of the horses died, she and her sister would drive into town to buy new boots and a ruffle for the

Sabbath. And if everything shone upon them and all the crops brought good prices, they added a few bits of furniture to their small supply, or bought more silver to hide away in the chest that would go to the sister that married first.

Which of them would come in for this chest Lena never troubled about. She would sit for long hours after the field was cleared, saying nothing, looking away into the horizon, perhaps tossing a pebble down the hill, listening for its echo in the ravine.

She did not even speculate on the way Una looked upon matters. Una was her sister; that was sufficient. One's right arm is always accompanied by one's left. Lena had not learned that left arms sometimes steal while right arms are vibrating under the handshake of friendship.

Sometimes Uncle Karl would get away from Lena and, striding over bog and hedge, dash into a neighboring farm, and there make trouble for the owner. At such times, Lena would lead him home, in the same unperturbed manner in which she drove the cows. Once a man had brought him back.

This man was Swedish, pale-faced, with a certain keenness of glance that gave one a suspicion that he had an occasional thought that did not run on farming. He was broad of shoulder, standing some six feet three. He had come to see Una many times after this. Standing by the door of an evening, he would turn his head and shoulders from side to side, looking first at one sister and then at the other. He had those pale, well-shaped lips that give the impression that they must be comfortable to the wearer. From time to time, he wetted them with a quick plunge of his tongue.

He always wore brown overalls, baggy at the knee, and lighter in color where he leaned on his elbows. The sisters had learned the first day that he was 'help' for the owner of the adjoining farm. They grunted their approval and asked him what wages he got. When he said a dollar and a half and board all through the Winter season, Una smiled upon him.

'Good pay,' she said, and offered him a glass of mulled wine.

Lena said nothing. Hands on hips, she watched him, or looked up into the sky. Lena was still young and the night yet appealed to her. She liked the Swede too. He was compact and big and 'well bred.' By this she meant what is meant when she said the same thing of a horse. He had quality – which meant the same thing through her fingers. And he was 'all right' in the same way soil is all right for securing profits. In other words, he was healthy and was making a living.

At first he had looked oftenest at Lena. Hers was the softer face of two faces as hard as stone. About her chin was a pointed excellence that might have meant that at times she could look kindly, might at times attain sweetness in her slow smile, a smile that drew lips reluctantly across very large fine teeth. It was a smile that in time might make one think more of these lips than of the teeth, instead of more of the teeth than the lips, as was as yet the case.

In Una's chin lurked a devil. It turned in under the lower lip secretively. Una's face was an unbroken block of calculation, saving where, upon her upper lip, a little down of hair fluttered.

Yet it gave one an uncanny feeling. It made one think of a tassel on a hammer.

Una had marked this Swede for her own. She went to all the trouble that was in her to give him the equivalent of the society girl's most fetching glances. Una let him sit where she stood, let him lounge when there was work to be done. Where she would have set anyone else to peeling potatoes, to him she offered wine or flat beer, black bread and sour cakes.

Lena did none of these things. She seemed to scorn him, she pretended to be indifferent to him, she looked past him. If she had been intelligent though, she would have looked through him.

For him her indifference was scorn, for him her quietness was disapproval, for him her unconcern was insult. Finally he left her alone, devoting his time to Una, calling for her often of a Sunday to take a long walk. Where to and why, it did not matter. To a festival at the church, to a pig killing, if one was going on a Sunday. Lena did not seem to mind. This was her purpose; she was by no means generous, she was by no means self-sacrificing. It simply never occurred to her that she could marry before her sister, who was the elder. In reality it was an impatience to be married that made her avoid Una's lover. As soon as Una was off her hands, then she, too, could think of marrying.

Una could not make her out at all. Sometimes she would call her to her and, standing arms akimbo, would stare at her for a good many minutes, so long that Lena would forget her and look off into the sky.

One day Una called Lena to her and asked her to make her mark at the bottom of a sheet of paper covered with hard cramped writing, Una's own.

'What is it?' asked Lena, taking the pen.

'Just saying that every other foot of this land is yours.'

'That you know already, eh?' Lena announced, putting the pen down. Una gave it back to her.

'I know it, but I want you to write it – that every other foot of land is mine, beginning with the second foot from the fence.'

Lena shrugged her shoulders. 'What for?'

'The lawyers want it.'

Lena signed her mark and laid down the pen. Presently she began to shell peas. All of a sudden she shook her head.

'I thought,' she said, 'that second foot was mine – what?' She thrust the pan down toward her knees and sat staring at Una with wide, suspicious eyes.

'Yah,' affirmed Una, who had just locked the paper up in a box.

Lena wrinkled her forehead, thereby bringing the red fringe a little nearer her eyes.

'But you made me sign it that it was you, hey?'

'Yah,' Una assented, setting the water on to boil for tea.

'Why?' inquired Una.

'To make more land,' Una replied, and grinned.

'More land?' queried Lena, putting the pan of peas upon the table and standing up. 'What do you mean?'

'More land for me,' Una answered complacently.

Lena could not understand and began to rub her hands. She picked up a pod and snapped it in her teeth.

'But I was satisfied,' she said, 'with the land as it was. I don't want more.'

'I do,' answered Una.

'Does it make me more?' Lena asked suspiciously, leaning a little forward.

'It makes you,' Una answered, 'nothing. Now you stay by me as helper –'

Then Lena understood. She stood stock still for a second. Suddenly she picked up the breadknife and, lurching forward, cried out: 'You take my land from me –'

Una dodged, grasped the hand with the knife, brought it down, took it away placidly, pushed Lena off and repeated: 'Now you work just the same, but for me – why you so angry?'

No tears came to Lena's help. And had they done so, they would have hissed against the flaming steel of her eyeballs. In a level tone thick with a terrible and sudden hate, she said: 'You know what you have done – eh? Yes, you have taken away the fruit trees from me, you have taken away the place where I worked for years, you have robbed me of my crops, you have stolen the harvest – that is well – but you have taken away from me the grave, too. The place where I live you have robbed me of and the place where I go when I die. I would have worked for you perhaps – but,' she struck her breast, 'when I die I die for myself.' Then she turned and left the house.

She went directly to the barn. Taking the two stallions out, she harnessed them to the carriage. With as little noise as possible she got them into the driveway. Then climbing in and securing the whip in one hand and the reins fast in the other, she cried aloud in a hoarse voice: 'Ahya you little dog. Watch me ride!' Then as Una came running to the door, Lena shouted back, turning in the trap: 'I take from you too.' And flinging the whip across the horses, she disappeared in a whirl of dust.

Una stood there shading her eyes with her hand. She had never seen Lena angry, therefore she thought she had gone mad as her uncle before her. That she had played Lena a dirty trick, she fully realized, but that Lena should realize it also, she had not counted on.

She wondered when Lena would come back with the horses. She even prepared a meal for two.

Lena did not come back. Una waited up till dawn. She was more frightened about the horses than she was about her sister; the horses represented six hundred dollars, while Lena only represented a relative. In the morning, she scolded Karl for giving mad blood to the family. Then toward the second evening, she waited for the Swede.

The evening passed as the others. The Swedish working man did not come.

Una was distracted. She called in a neighbor and set the matter before him. He gave her some legal advice and left her bewildered.

Finally, at the end of that week, because neither horses nor Lena had appeared, and also because of the strange absence of the man who had been making love to her for some weeks, Una reported the matter to the local police. And ten days later they located the horses. The man driving them said that they had been sold to him by a young Polish woman who passed through his farm with a tall Swedish man late at night. She said that she had tried to sell them that day at a fair and had been unable to part with them, and finally let them go to him at a low price. He added that he had paid three hundred dollars for them. Una bought them back at the figure, from hard earned savings, both of her own and Lena's.

Then she waited. A sour hatred grew up within her and she moved about from acre to acre with her hired help like some great thing made of wood.

But she changed in her heart as the months passed. At times she almost regretted what she had done. After all, Lena had been quiet and hard working and her kin. It had been Lena, too, who had best quieted Karl. Without her he stormed and stamped about the house, and of late had begun to accuse her of having killed her sister.

Then one day Lena appeared carrying something on her arms, swaying it from side to side while the Swede hitched a fine mare to the barn door. Up the walk came Lena, singing, and behind her came her man.

Una stood still, impassible, quiet. As Lena reached her, she uncovered the bundle and held the baby up to her.

'Kiss it,' she said. Without a word, Una bent at the waist and kissed it.

'Thank you,' Lena said as she replaced the shawl. 'Now you have left your mark. Now you have signed.' She smiled.

The Swedish fellow was a little browned from the sun. He took his cap off, and stood there grinning awkwardly.

Lena pushed in at the door and sat down.

Una followed her. Behind Una came the father.

Karl was heard singing and stamping overhead. 'Give her some molasses water and little cakes,' he shouted, putting his head down through the trap door, and burst out laughing.

Una brought three glasses of wine. Leaning forward, she poked her finger into the baby's cheek to make it smile. 'Tell me about it,' she said.

Lena began: 'Well, then I got him,' she pointed to the awkward father. 'And I put him in behind me and I took him to town and I marry him. And I explain to him. I say: "She took my land from me, the flowers and the fruit and the green things. And she took the grave from me where I should lie –"'

And in the end they looked like fine horses, but one of them was a bit spirited.

Looking for a Rain God

Bessie Head

It is lonely at the lands where the people go to plough. These lands are vast clearings in the bush, and the wild bush is lonely too. Nearly all the lands are within walking distance from the village. In some parts of the bush where the underground water is very near the surface, people made little rest camps for themselves and dug shallow wells to quench their thirst while on their journey to their own lands. They experienced all kinds of things once they left the village. They could rest at shady watering places full of lush, tangled trees with delicate pale-gold and purple wild flowers springing up between soft green moss and the children could hunt around for wild figs and any berries that might be in season. But from 1958, a seven-year drought fell upon the land and even the watering places began to look as dismal as the dry open thorn-bush country; the leaves of the trees curled up and withered; the moss became dry and hard and, under the shade of the tangled trees, the ground turned a powdery black and white, because there was no rain. People said rather humorously that if you tried to catch the rain in a cup it would only fill a teaspoon. Towards the beginning of the seventh year of drought, the summer had become an anguish to live through. The air was so dry and moisture-free that it burned the skin. No one knew what to do to escape the heat and tragedy was in the air. At the beginning of that summer, a number of men just went out of their homes and hung themselves to death from trees. The majority of the people had lived off crops, but for two years past they had all returned from the lands with only their rolled-up skin blankets and cooking utensils. Only the charlatans, incanters, and witch-doctors made a pile of money during this time because people were always turning to them in desperation for little talismans and herbs to rub on the plough for the crops to grow and the rain to fall.

The rains were late that year. They came in early November, with a promise of good rain. It wasn't the full, steady downpour of the years of good rain, but thin, scanty, misty rain. It softened the earth and a rich growth of green things sprang up everywhere for the animals to eat. People were called to the village kgotla to hear the proclamation of the beginning of the ploughing season; they stirred themselves and whole families began to move off to the lands to plough.

The family of the old man, Mokgobja, were among those who left early for the lands. They had a donkey cart and piled everything onto it, Mokgobja – who was over seventy years old; two little girls, Neo and Boseyong; their mother Tiro and an unmarried sister, Nesta; and the father and supporter of the family, Ramadi, who drove the donkey cart. In the rush of the first hope of rain, the man, Ramadi, and the two women, cleared the land of thorn-bush and then hedged their vast ploughing area with this same thorn-bush to protect the future crop from the goats they had brought along for milk. They cleared out and deepened the old well with its pool of muddy water and still in this light, misty rain, Ramadi inspanned two oxen and turned the earth over with a hand plough.

The land was ready and ploughed, waiting for the crops. At night, the earth was alive with insects singing and rustling about in search of food. But suddenly, by mid-November, the rain fled away; the rain-clouds fled away and left the sky bare. The sun danced dizzily in the sky, with a strange cruelty. Each day the land was covered in a haze of mist as the sun sucked up the last drop of moisture out of the earth. The family sat down in despair, waiting and waiting. Their hopes had run so high; the goats had started producing milk, which they had eagerly poured on their porridge, now they ate plain porridge with no milk. It was impossible to plant the corn, maize, pumpkin and water-melon seeds in the dry earth. They sat the whole day in the shadow of the huts and even stopped thinking, for the rain had fled away. Only the children, Neo and Boseyong, were quite happy in their little girl world. They carried on with their game of making house like their mother and chattered to each other in light, soft tones. They made children from sticks around which they tied rags, and scolded them severely in an exact imitation of their own mother. Their voices could be heard scolding the day long: 'You stupid thing, when I send you to draw water, why do you spill half of it out of the bucket!' 'You stupid thing! Can't you mind the porridge-pot without letting the porridge burn!' And then they would beat the rag-dolls on their bottoms with severe expressions.

The adults paid no attention to this; they did not even hear the funny chatter; they sat waiting for rain; their nerves were stretched to breaking-point willing the rain to fall out of the sky. Nothing was important, beyond that. All their animals had been sold during the bad years to purchase food, and of all their herd only two goats were left. It was the women of the family who finally broke under the strain of waiting for rain. It was really the two women who caused the death of the little girls. Each night they started a weird, high-pitched wailing that began on a low, mournful note and whipped up to a frenzy. Then they would stamp their feet and shout as though they had lost their heads. The men sat quiet and self-controlled; it was important for men to maintain their self-control at all times but their nerve was breaking too. They knew the women were haunted by the starvation of the coming year.

Finally, an ancient memory stirred in the old man, Mokgobja. When he was very young and the customs of the ancestors still ruled the land, he had been witness to a rain-making ceremony. And he came alive a little, struggling to recall the details which had been buried by years and years of prayer in a Christian church. As soon as the mists cleared a little, he began consulting in whispers with his youngest son, Ramadi. There was, he said, a certain rain god who accepted only the sacrifice of the bodies of children. Then the rain would fall; then the crops would grow, he said. He explained the ritual and as he talked, his memory became a conviction and he began to talk with unshakeable authority. Ramadi's nerves were smashed by the nightly wailing of the women and soon the two men began whispering with the two women. The children continued their game: 'You stupid thing! How could you have lost the money on the way to the shop! You must have been playing again!'

After it was all over and the bodies of the two little girls had been spread across the land, the rain did not fall. Instead, there was a deathly silence at night and the devouring heat of the sun by day. A terror, extreme and deep, overwhelmed the whole family. They packed, rolling up their skin blankets and pots, and fled back to the village.

People in the village soon noted the absence of the two little girls. They had died at the lands and were buried there, the family said. But people noted their ashen, terror-stricken faces and a murmur arose. What had killed the children, they wanted to know? And the family replied that they had just died. And people said amongst themselves that it was strange that the two deaths had occurred at the same time. And there was a feeling of great unease at the unnatural looks of the family. Soon the police came around. The family told them the same story of death and burial at the lands. They did not know what the children had died of. So the police asked to see the graves. At this, the mother of the children broke down and told everything.

Throughout the terrible summer the story of the children hung like a dark cloud of sorrow over the village, and the sorrow was not assuaged when the old man and Ramadi were sentenced to death for ritual murder. All they had on the statute books was that ritual murder was against the law and must be stamped out with the death penalty. The subtle story of strain and starvation and breakdown was inadmissible evidence at court; but all the people who lived off crops knew in their hearts that only a hair's breadth had saved them from sharing a fate similar to that of the Mokgobja family. They could have killed something to make the rain fall.

A Visit from the Footbinder

Emily Prager

'I shall have the finest burial tomb in China if it's the last thing I do,' Lady Guo Guo muttered triumphantly to herself. It was mid-afternoon at the height of the summer, and the Pavilion of Coolness was dark and still. She tottered over to the scrolls of snow scenes which lined the walls and meditated on them for a moment to relieve herself from the heat.

'Sixteen summers in the making, sixteen memorable summers and finally ready for decor. Oh, how I've waited for this moment. I think blue for the burial chamber overall, or should it be green? Ah, Pleasure Mouse, do you think blue for Mummy's burial chamber or green?'

Pleasure Mouse, aged six, second and youngest daughter of Lady Guo Guo, pondered this as she danced a series of jigs around her mother. 'Blue would be lovely on you, Mummy, especially in death. Green, a bit sad and unflattering, I think.'

'You are so right, Pleasure Mouse. Green reeks of decay. Such an unerring sense of taste in one so young – I see a fabulous marriage in your future. In two or three seasons, after Tiger Mouse has been wed,' Lady Guo Guo looked away. 'Revered Mummy,' Pleasure Mouse was leaping up and down and tugging at her mother's very long sleeves, 'at what hour will the footbinder come tomorrow? How long does it take? Can I wear the little shoes right away? Will I be all grown up then like Tiger Mouse?'

Lady Guo Guo shuffled quickly toward the teakwood table on which lay the blueprints of the pavilions erected to date. Pleasure Mouse ran in front of her and darted and pounced at her playfully like a performing mongoose at his colleague the performing snake.

As a result of this frolicking, Lady Guo Guo lost her

balance and, grabbing on to the edge of the table to steady herself, she snapped angrily, 'No answers, Pleasure Mouse! Because of your immodest behaviour I will give no answers to your indelicate questions. Go now. I am very displeased.'

'Yes, Mummy, I am sorry, Mummy,' said Pleasure Mouse, much chastened, and, after a solemn but ladylike bow, she fled from the Pavilion of Coolness.

Pleasure Mouse raced across the white-hot courtyard, past the evaporating Felicitous Rebirth Fishpond, and into the Red Dust Pavilion, which contained the apartments of her thirteen-year-old sister, Tiger Mouse. Inside, all was light or shadow. There were no shades of grey. The pungent aroma of jasmine sachet hung on the hot, dry air like an insecure woman on the arm of her lover. As usual, Tiger Mouse was kneeling on the gaily tiled floor, dozens of open lacquer boxes spread around her, counting her shoes.

As Pleasure Mouse burst into the chamber, Tiger Mouse glanced up at her and said haughtily, 'I have one thousand pairs of tiny satin shoes. If you don't believe me, you can count them for yourself. Go ahead,' she said with a sweeping gesture, 'count them. Go on!' Wavering slightly, hair ornaments askew, she got to her feet. Then she went on: 'I have the tiniest feet in the prefecture, no longer than newborn kittens. Look. Look!'

Tiger Mouse toddled intently to a corner of the chamber in which stood the charcoal brazier used for heating in winter. Now, of course, it lay unused, iron-cold in the stifling heat. For a moment, she encircled it with her arms and rested her cheek and breast against the cool metal. Then she reached beneath it and amid a chorus of protesting squeaks brought out two newborn kittens, one in each hand, which she then placed beside each of her pointy little feet.

'Come,' she said. 'Look,' and she raised her skirt. Pleasure Mouse ran and squatted down before her. It was true. The newborn kittens, eyes glued shut, ears pasted to the sides of their heads, swam helplessly on the tiled floor, peeping piteously for milk. They were far more lively than Tiger Mouse's feet but certainly no bigger. Pleasure Mouse was terribly impressed.

'It is true what you say, Older Sister, and wonderful. No bigger than newborn kittens –'

'No *longer* than newborn kittens,' Tiger Mouse barked.

'Indeed,' Pleasure Mouse responded in a conciliatory tone and then, by way of a jest to lighten the moment, added, 'Take care the mother cat does not retrieve your feet.' Pleasure Mouse laughed sweetly and ran trippingly alongside Tiger Mouse as the latter, smiling faintly, wavered back to her many shoes and knelt before them.

'Tiger Mouse,' Pleasure Mouse twirled around in embarrassment as she spoke, unsure of the consequences her questions might elicit, 'the footbinder comes tomorrow to bind my feet. Will it hurt? What will they look like afterwards? Please tell me.'

'Toads.'

'What?'

'My feet are like the perfect Golden Lotus. But yours, horned toads. Big, fat ones.'

'Oh, Tiger Mouse –'

'And it didn't hurt me in the least. It only hurts if you're a liar and a cheat or a sorcerer. Unworthy. Spoiled. Discourteous. And don't think that you can try on my shoes after, because you can't. They are mine. All one thousand pairs.'

'Yes, Tiger Mouse.' Pleasure Mouse dashed behind her and snatched up one pair of the tiny shoes and concealed them in the long sleeve of her tunic. 'I must go for my music lesson now, Older Sister,' she said as she hurried toward the chamber door. She stopped just short of exiting and turned and bowed. 'Please excuse me.'

'But perhaps,' said Tiger Mouse, ignoring her request, 'the pain is so great that one's sentiments are smashed like egg shells. Perhaps for many seasons, one cries out for death and cries unheeded, pines for it and yearns for it. Why should I tell you what no one told me?'

'Because I'd tell you?' answered Pleasure Mouse. But Tiger Mouse went back to counting her shoes. The audience was over.

Pleasure Mouse scampered out of the Red Dust Pavilion, past the evaporating Felicitous Rebirth Fishpond, and through the gate into the recently completed Perfect Afterlife Garden. When she reached the Bridge of Piquant Memory, she stopped to catch her breath and watch as her mother's maids watered the ubiquitous jasmine with the liquid of fermented fish in hopes that this might make it last the summer. The stench was overpowering, threatening to sicken, and Pleasure Mouse sped away along the Stream of No Regrets, through the Heavenly Thicket and into the Meadow of One Hundred Orchids, where her friends, the One Hundred Orchid Painters, sat capturing the glory of the blossom for all time.

Aged Fen Wen, the master painter, looked up from his silken scroll and smiled. For sixteen years, he had laboured on Lady Guo Guo's burial tomb, at first in charge of screens and calligraphic scrolls, and now, since they were done, of wall hangings, paintings, window mats and ivory sculpture. He had watched as Pleasure Mouse grew from a single brushstroke to an intricate design, and though he was but an artisan, he considered himself an uncle to her.

For her part, Pleasure Mouse adored Fen Wen. No matter where the old man was at work on the great estate, no matter how many leagues away, as soon as she awoke in the morning she would run and find him. During the winter when her family returned to the city, she missed him terribly, for although she loved her father, she rarely saw him. With Fen Wen there was no need to observe formalities.

Fen Wen was sitting, as was each of the ninety-nine other Orchid Painters, on an intricately carved three-legged stool before an ebony table on which lay a scroll and brushes. There were one hundred such tables, and in front of each grew a single tree, each one supporting an orchid vine, each vine bearing one perfect blossom. The trees grew in twenty rows of five across, and aged Fen Wen was giving leaf corrections at the southwestern corner of the meadow, where Pleasure Mouse now found him and, without further ado, leapt into his lap.

'Venerable Fen Wen,' she said as she snuggled into his chest and looked deep into his eyes, 'guess what.'

Fen Wen wrinkled his Buddha-like brow and thought. 'The emperor has opened an acting school in his pear garden?' he said finally.

'No.'

'You have fallen in love with an imitator of animal noises?'

'No, no,' Pleasure Mouse giggled happily.

'I give up,' said Fen Wen, and Pleasure Mouse wiggled out of his lap and skipped in place as she related her news.

'The footbinder is coming tomorrow to bind my feet. And afterwards I shall wear tiny shoes just like these,' she produced the pair she had stolen from Tiger Mouse, waved them before Fen Wen, then concealed them again, 'and I will be all grown up –'

Pleasure Mouse halted abruptly. Fen Wen's great droopy eyes had filled with tears, and the Orchid Painters around him modestly looked away.

'Ah,' he sighed softly. 'Then we won't see you any more.'

'No. What do you mean? Why do you say that?' Pleasure Mouse grabbed on to Fen Wen's tunic and searched deeply into his eyes.

'At first, of course, you will not be able to walk at all, and then later when you have healed, you may make it as far as the front Moon Gate, but, alas, Pleasure Mouse, no farther. Never as far as this Meadow. Never as far. They won't want you to. Once your –'

'Won't be able to walk?' said Pleasure Mouse quizzically. 'What do you mean? Lady Guo Guo walks. Tiger Mouse walks . . .'

Now began a silence as aged Fen Wen and the ninety-nine other Orchid Painters turned glumly toward the east, leaving Pleasure Mouse, aged six, second and youngest daughter of Lady Guo Guo, alone and possessed of her first conceptual thought. Past experience joined with present and decocted future. Nuggets of comprehension, like grains of rice in a high wind, swirled behind her eyes, knocked together and blew apart. Only this softly spoken phrase was heard on earth.

'They cannot run,' she said, 'but I can.' And she ran, through the Meadow of One Hundred Orchids, down the Path of Granted Wishes, and out of the Sun Gate into the surrounding countryside.

Just outside the market town of Catchow, a mile or so down the Dragon Way near the vast estate of the prefect Lord Guo Guo, lay situated the prosperous Five Enjoyments Tea House. On this spot one afternoon in the tenth century, three hundred years before the tea house was built and our story began, a Taoist priest and a Buddhist nun were strolling together and came upon a beggar. Filthy and poor, he lay by the side of the road and called out to them. 'Come over here. I am dying. I have only this legacy to leave.' The beggar was waving something and the Taoist priest and the Buddhist nun moved closer to see what it was.

'Look,' said the beggar, 'it is a piece of the very silk with which the emperor bade a dancing girl swaddle her feet that they might look like points of the moon sickle. She then danced in the centre of a six-foot lotus fashioned out of gold and decorated with jewels.' The beggar fell backward, exhausted by his tale, and gasped for breath. The Taoist priest and the Buddhist nun examined the dirty, bloody, ragged scrap of cloth and glanced at each other with great scepticism.

'Ah yes. It is an interesting way to step from Existence into Nonexistence, is it not?' said the Buddhist nun.

'Indeed,' replied the Taoist priest. 'So much easier to escape Desire and sidle closer to Immortality when one can follow only a very few paths. But alas, in time, this too will pass.'

There was a rattle in the beggar's throat then, and his eyes rolled upward and grasping the scrap of silk, he died.

The Taoist priest and the Buddhist nun murmured some words of prayer over the beggar's body, linked arms and continued their travels. The ragged scrap of bloody cloth fluttered to the ground and was transformed by the Goddess of Resignation into a precious stone that lay at that very spot until the year 1266, when it was discovered and made into a ring by the famous courtesan Honey Tongue, star attraction of The Five Enjoyments Tea House, which had been built nearby some years before.

Pleasure Mouse, taking extreme care not to be seen, scrambled up the back stairs of The Five Enjoyments Tea House and sneaked into the luxurious apartments of her father's good friend, the famous courtesan, Honey Tongue. She startled the beauteous lady as she sat before her mirror tinting her nails with pink balsam leaves crushed in alum. 'Oh!' exclaimed Honey Tongue. 'Why, it's Pleasure Mouse, isn't it? Sit down, little one, you're out of breath. What brings you here?'

Pleasure Mouse collapsed on a brocade cushion and burst into tears. The beauteous lady floated to her side and hugged her warmly to her perfumed breast. 'Oh dear,' crooned Honey Tongue, rocking back and forth, 'oh dear oh dear oh dear,' until finally Pleasure Mouse was able to speak: 'Tomorrow, the footbinder comes to bind my feet and –'

Honey Tongue brought her hands to her mouth and laughed behind them. She rose from Pleasure Mouse's cushion and, still laughing, wafted back to her seat before her mirror. She fiddled for a moment with her hair ornaments and began to apply the stark white Buddha adornment to her face and afterward the deep-rose blush.

As all this seemed to contain great meaning, Pleasure Mouse ceased speaking and ran to her side, watching in the mirror everything the lovely lady did. When she was done plucking her eyebrows and smoothing on the final drop of hair oil, she smiled the loveliest of sunny smiles and said, 'It's a bargain, Pleasure Mouse. The pain goes away after two years, and then you have a weapon you never dreamed of. Now, run along home before someone sees you here.'

Pleasure Mouse did as she was told, but as she was speeding along the Dragon Way, trying to reach the eastern Sun Gate of the estate before she was seen, she had the bad fortune to run smack into the sedan chair procession of her father's older sister, Lao Bing. Her old auntie had come all the way from the city for the footbinding, and when she peered out of the window of her sedan chair and saw Pleasure Mouse, she bellowed in an imperious tone, 'Halt!'

The bearers halted abruptly and set the sedan chair down in the middle of the Dragon Way. An enormous donkey cart, that of the night-soil collector, which had been following a few lengths behind the procession, now was forced to halt also, and a vicious verbal battle ensued between the chair bearers and the night-soil collector and his men as to who had the right of way. Lao Bing paid no attention to this mêlée. She opened the door of the sedan chair and cried out, 'All right, Pleasure Mouse, I see you. Come over here this minute.'

Pleasure Mouse ran to the sedan chair and scampered inside. As she closed the door, Lao Bing bellowed, 'Drive on!' and the bearers stopped quarrelling with the collector, hoisted the sedan chair poles onto their knobby-muscled shoulders, and continued in a silent run to the estate.

The sedan chair rocked like a rowboat on a storm-tossed sea. Pleasure Mouse began to feel queasy inside the dark box. The odour of Lao Bing's hair oil permeated the heavy brocades, and the atmosphere was cloying. The old one's hair ornaments jiggled in emphasis as she spoke.

'Really, Pleasure Mouse, young maidens of good family are not allowed outdoors, much less outside the estate grounds. Oh, if your father knew I had found you on the Dragon Way . . .'

'Dearest Auntie,' entreated Pleasure Mouse, 'please don't tell. I only thought since the footbinder is coming tomorrow and I'll no longer be able to –'

'Footbinder?' Lao Bing seemed perturbed. 'What footbinder? You don't mean to tell me your mother has *hired* a footbinder for tomorrow?' Pleasure Mouse nodded.

'Really, that woman spends like a spoiled concubine!' Lao Bing peeked through the curtain on the window and sighed in resignation. 'All right, Pleasure Mouse, we are inside the Sun Gate now. You may get down. Halt!' The bearers halted and Lao Bing opened the door.

'Auntie?' Pleasure Mouse hesitated before the door. 'What is it like?'

Lao Bing mulled the question over for a moment and then replied briskly, 'It is something a woman must endure in order to make a good marriage. No more. No less, Pleasure Mouse. If you wish to live at court, you must have tiny feet. Logic, indubitable logic.'

'And does it hurt, Lao Bing?' Pleasure Mouse gazed stoically into her aunt's eyes and prepared herself for the reply. The old lady never minced words.

'Beauty is the stillbirth of suffering, every woman knows that. Now scamper away, little mouse, and dream your girlish dreams, for tomorrow you will learn some secret things that will make you feel old.'

Lao Bing closed the door of the sedan chair and gave the order: 'Drive on!' Pleasure Mouse circled the Meadow of One Hundred Orchids, traversed The Heavenly Thicket, and made her way to the recently constructed Avenue of Lifelong Misconceptions, where she passed the afternoon contemplating her future footsize.

Lady Guo Guo was receiving in her burial chamber. It was bleak in the dense stone edifice, dim, musty and airless, but it was cool and the flaming torches affixed to the walls gave off a flickering, dangerous light. A party of silk weavers from Shantung milled nervously in one corner while their agent haggled with Lady Guo Guo over the quantity of mouse-vein-blue silk. In another corner, the head caterer waited to discuss the banquet of the dead and dodged attempts by a group of nosy flower arrangers to guess the menu. There were poetry chanters, trainers of performing insects, literary men – throngs of humanity of every occupation crammed into the burial chamber and its anteroom, hoping to be hired for a day's labour. And many had been. And many were. One local gluemaker had quite literally made his fortune off Lady Guo Guo in the last sixteen years. He had retired early, well-fed and happy. And he was but one among many.

It was through this teeming mass of gilders, cutlers, jugglers, sackmakers, pork butchers and pawnshop owners, that Lao Bing now made her way preceded by three servants who, rather noisily and brutishly, made a path. Lady Guo Guo, distracted by the commotion, looked up from her bargaining, recognized her sister-in-law, and hurried to greet her.

'Welcome, venerable husband's sister, to my recently completed burial chamber. Majestic, is it not? I shall enter the afterlife like a princess wearing a gown of,' Lady Guo Guo snapped the bolt of silk and it unrolled like a snake across the cold stone floor, 'this blue silk. My colour, I think you'll admit. Thank goodness you have come with all your years of wisdom behind you,' Lao Bing sniffed audibly, 'for I need your advice, Lao Bing. Do we do the wall hangings in the blue with a border in a green of new apples or a green of old lizards who have recently sluffed their skin? Question two: Who shall do my death mask and who my ancestor portrait? Should the same man do both?'

'Old lizards and different men,' said Lao Bing decisively,

and tottered over to a sandalwood stool and sat on it. 'Little Sister,' she began, a note of warning in her voice, 'these days the lord, your husband, reminds me of a thunderclap in clothes. Day and night the creditors camp outside the door of the prefecture. He asks why you do not use the rents from the rooming houses you inherited from your father to pay these merchants?'

'What? And deplete my family's coffers? The lord, my husband, is as tight with cash as the strings on a courtesan's purse, Lao Bing, and no tighter. Do not deceive yourself.'

'Well, really,' said Lao Bing, her sensibilities offended, and, her message delivered, abruptly changed the subject. 'They say that the fallow deer sold in the market is actually donkey flesh. It's a dreadful scandal. The city is buzzing with it. And as if that weren't enough –' Lao Bing lowered her voice, rose from her seat, and ushered Lady Guo Guo away from the throngs and down into the depression in the vast stone floor where her coffin would eventually lie. 'As if that weren't enough,' Lao Bing continued, sotto voce, 'the emperor is using his concubines to hunt rabbits.'

Lady Guo Guo was horror-struck. 'What? Instead of dogs?'

Lao Bing nodded solemnly.

'But they cannot run.'

'Ah, well, that's the amusement in it, don't you see? They cannot possibly keep up with the horses. They stumble and fall –'

Lady Guo Guo swayed from side to side. 'No more please. I feel faint.'

'You are too delicate, younger brother's wife.'

'For this world but not for the next.' Lady Guo Guo patted the lip of the depression to emphasize her point.

'Hmm, yes,' said Lao Bing, 'if it is up to you. All of which brings me to the subject of tomorrow's footbinding. Pleasure Mouse tells me you've *hired* a footbinder.'

'Really, Lao Bing, expense is no object where my daughter's feet –'

'I have no concern with the expense, Little Sister. It is simply that the Guo Guo women have been binding their daughters' feet themselves for centuries. To pay an outsider to perform such an intimate, such a traditional, such an honourable and serious act is an outrage, a travesty, a shirking of responsibility, unlucky, too arrogant and a dreadful loss of face.'

'Lao Bing,' Lady Guo Guo climbed out of the depression with the help of a sackmaker who hurried over to ingratiate himself. 'You are like an old donkey on the Dragon Way, unable to forge a new path, stubbornly treading the muddy ruts of the previous donkey and cart. This footbinder is a specialist, an artist renowned throughout the district. And what is more important in this mortal world, I'm sure you'll agree, is not who does or does not do the binding, but the size of Pleasure Mouse's feet once it's done.'

Lao Bing clapped her hands, and her servants appeared by her side, hoisted her out of the depression and set her down once again on the cold stone floor. Her hair ornaments spun with the impact. 'Very well,' she said after some moments of icy reflection. 'But let us hope that with your modern ways you have not offended any household spirits.'

A breeze of fear gusted across Lady Guo Guo's features. 'I am not a fool, Lao Bing,' she said quietly. 'In the last few days I have burned enough incense to propitiate the entire netherworld. I have begged the blessing of ancestors so long departed they failed to recognize our family name and had to be reminded. The geomancer claimed he had never seen anything like it – before he collapsed from exhaustion.'

'And he is sure about tomorrow?' Lao Bing asked, and then regretted it.

'Really, Lao Bing.' Lady Guo Guo turned on a tiny heel and scurried back to her bargaining table. With a snap of her fingers, she summoned two maids and instructed them to show Lao Bing to her apartments in the Red Dust Pavilion. The old lady, suddenly fatigued by her journey, waddled slowly over to her sister-in-law's side and said gently, 'Forgive me, Little Sister. It is a festival fraught with sentiments, worse this time perhaps because it is my perky Pleasure Mouse.'

But Lady Guo Guo had returned to her business. 'I'll take the green of old lizards,' she was saying to the silk weavers' agent, 'at three cash per yard and not a penny more.' Haggling began anew and echoed off the great stone walls. Lao Bing departed, preceded by her servants, who elbowed her way into the crowd, which parted for a moment to admit her and then closed behind her again. Just like, thought Lady Guo Guo, a python who swallows whole its prey.

In the hot, dry centre of the oven-baked night, Pleasure Mouse tossed and turned and glowed with tiny drops of baby sweat. Ordinarily, the nightly strumming of the zither players out in the courtyard would have long since lulled her to sleep, but not this night. She was far too excited.

She sat up on her lacquered bed, crossed her legs, and removed from beneath her pillow the tiny pair of shoes she had stolen from her sister. She stroked them for a moment, deep red satin with sky-blue birds and lime-green buds embroidered over all, and then placed them on the coverlet in the strongest of rays of blue moonlight.

'How sweet,' she murmured to herself, 'how beauteous. Soon I will embroider some for myself and I will choose . . . cats and owls. So tiny, I do not see how –'

And she glanced around to make sure she was alone and unseen, and stealthily picked up one shoe and tried to slip it on her foot. But it would not fit, in any way whatsoever. Most of her toes, her heel and half of her foot spilled over the sides. She was very disappointed. 'Perhaps my feet are already too big,' she sighed aloud, and might have tried once more like panicked birds who fly into the window mat and though they've gained no exit, fly again, but just then the jagged sound of breaking glass shattered her reverie, and up she sprang and hid the tiny shoes beneath her pillow.

'Who goes there?' she cried, and ran to the door of her chamber.

'Oh, great heavens, Pleasure Mouse, it's I,' came the whispered reply, and Pleasure Mouse sighed with relief and slipped into the corridor. There, crisscrossed by moonlight, on her knees before a broken vial, her father's concubine, Warm Milk, aged nineteen and great with child for lo these six long moons, looked up at her and wept. 'Oh, Pleasure Mouse,' she managed through her tears, 'I've ruined the decoction. I'll never get more dog flies now in time, or earthworms, for that matter. It took weeks to collect the ingredients and I've dropped them. It's my legs. They're swollen like dead horses in the mud. And as for my feet, well, they're no longer of this earth, Pleasure Mouse.' Warm Milk rolled off her knees and sat squarely on the floor, her eyes tightly shut and soft moans of agony escaping her lips as she stretched her legs out in front of her. Pleasure Mouse stared at her opulent stomach, which looked like a giant peach protruding through Warm Milk's bedclothes and wondered what creature was inside. Warm Milk bent over and began to massage her legs. Her tiny white-bandaged feet stuck out beyond the hem of her nightgown like standards of surrender at a miniature battle. 'They cannot bear the weight of two, Pleasure Mouse, but never say I said so. Promise?'

Pleasure Mouse nodded solemnly. 'Promise,' she replied, and examined Warm Milk's feet out of the corner of her eyes.

'They stink, Pleasure Mouse, that's the worst of it, like a pork butcher's hands at the end of a market day. It frightens me, Pleasure Mouse, but never say I said so. Promise?'

Pleasure Mouse nodded furiously. She would have liked to speak but when she tried, no voice was forthcoming. Her little girl's body had begun to contract with a terrible heat and in the pit of her stomach, feelings cavorted like the boxers she had heard of at the pleasure grounds.

Warm Milk leaned back on her hands and was silent for a moment. Her waist-length blue-black hair fell about her swollen little body and gleamed in the moonlight. Her flat, round face was blue-white, as pale and ghostlike as pure white jade. So too her hands.

'I was going to the shrine of the Moon Goddess to beg her for a boy. The decoction,' she sat up and gestured at the oozy pink puddle that was beginning to travel along the corridor floor, 'was to drink during the supplication. They say it always works, a male child is assured. Perhaps –' Warm Milk cupped her hands in the pink slime and brought it to her lips.

'No,' cried Pleasure Mouse, horrified at such intimacy with dirt. 'Please don't. You will be sick. Tomorrow I will run and find you many spiders and new dog flies too!' Warm Milk smiled gratefully at the little girl. 'Will you, Pleasure Mouse?' she asked. And Pleasure Mouse remembered.

'Oh, no, I can't,' she cried, blushing deeply. Her slanted eyes welled up with tears like tiny diamonds in the blue moonlight. 'Tomorrow, the footbinder comes to bind my feet and –'

'You shan't be running anywhere.' Warm Milk sighed resignedly and sucked the liquid from the palms of her hands. 'What bad fortune, Pleasure Mouse, for us both, as it turns out. For us both. But never say I said so.'

'Where are your toes?' Pleasure Mouse asked suddenly and without advance thought. It was just that she had glanced at Warm Milk's feet and finally realized what was different about them.

'My what?' asked Warm Milk nervously.

'Your toes.' Pleasure Mouse squatted down before the bandaged feet and pointed a tiny finger at them. 'I have five toes. You have one. Did they cut the others off?' Her eyes were wide with terror.

'No.' Warm Milk pulled her nightgown over her feet. 'No, of course not.'

'Well, what happened to them?' Pleasure Mouse looked directly into Warm Milk's kind black eyes and awaited an answer.

Warm Milk dropped her head and basked for a moment in the blue moonlight. Out in the courtyard, the zither players were at their height, their instruments warm and responsive, their male hearts carried away by the loveliness of the tune. At length, Warm Milk spoke.

'When I was but five seasons old, the elegance of my carriage and the delicacy of my stature were already known far and wide. And so my mother, on the counsel of my father, bound my feet, which was an unusual occurrence for a maid of my then lowly peasant status. I could not run. I could not play. The other girls made mockery of my condition. But when I was ten, your father spied my little shrew-nosed feet and bought me from my father for his honourable concubine. Beneath your venerable father's wing I have nestled healthfully and prosperously for many seasons but never so happily as when I see, from the heights of my sedan chair, my big-footed playmates now turned flower-drum girls hawking their wanton wares by the river's edge.'

Warm Milk laughed modestly. 'Do you understand me, Pleasure Mouse?' Pleasure Mouse nodded, but she wasn't sure. 'Yes, Honourable Concubine, but about your toes, where –' She began again but was interrupted by the appearance of six horrified maids who should have been on duty throughout the pavilion but who, because of the closeness of the evening, had ventured into the courtyard to watch the zither players, and had quite forgotten their charges in the romance of the moonlight and song.

The corridor rang with noises of reproach and then, like ants with a cake crumb, four of the maids quickly lifted up the concubine Warm Milk and bore her away to her apartments. The remaining two hurried Pleasure Mouse into her chamber and into her bed.

'I want my dolly,' said Pleasure Mouse mournfully, and the maid brought it to her. The big rag doll, fashioned for her by aged Fen Wen, with the lovely hand-painted face of the Moon Goddess, black hair of spun silk, and masterfully embroidered robes, came to her anxious mistress with open arms. Pleasure Mouse hugged her close and sniffed deeply at her silken hair. Then she slid her hand under the pillow, pulled out the tiny shoes and slipped them on the dolly's rag feet. After a bit of stuffing and pushing, the shoes fitted perfectly. And Spring Rain, for that was the dolly's name, looked so lady-like and harmonious of spirit in the tiny shoes, that Pleasure Mouse forgot her fears and soon was sound asleep.

The footbinder was late. Already it was two hours past cock-crow, and the courtyard outside the Temple of Two Thousand Ancestors was buzzing with anticipation and excitement. The man with the performing fish had arrived early and so was understandably perturbed about the wait. So too the tellers of obscene stories and the kiteflyer. Had it been another season, they might have chatted away the time, but it was mid-summer and as the hours dragged by, the day grew hotter and the energy for physical performance ebbed slowly away. The zither players were doing their best to keep up spirits, strumming at first soothingly and then rousingly in celebration of the occasion. Hands holding fans wafted back and forth in tempo to the music, pausing only to pluck cloying hair and clothing from damp and heated skin.

Inside the dark, hot temple, Lady Guo Guo stamped her

tiny foot. The din from the courtyard resounded through the walls, and she was dreadfully embarrassed before her ancestors. The geomancer, a thin, effeminate young man, shook his head and wrists.

'The propitious hour is upon us, Lady. After it passes, I cannot be responsible for the consequences.'

Lao Bing, suffering mightily from the heat and certainly tired of waiting, concurred, 'Really, Little Sister, we must get on with it. This is exactly what happens when you pay an outsider – oh!' Lao Bing, frustrated beyond words, ceased speaking and fanned herself wildly.

Before the altar, Pleasure Mouse sat on a stool with her feet soaking in a broth of monkey bones. She stared up at the portraits of her most recently departed ancestors, solemn in the yellow light of the prayer candles. Occasionally, her eyes travelled about the walls of the great chamber and met those of hundreds of other ancestors whom she had never known in life and of whom she had never heard.

Just after cock-crow, she had entered the temple with the female members of her family, she had prayed to the Little-Footed Miss for the plumpest and softest and finest of Lotus Hooks. You could, Lao Bing informed her, end up with either Long Hairpins, Buddha's Heads or Red Cocoons. It all depended on the expertise of the binding, the favour of the ancestral and household spirits, and the propitiousness of the hour at which the feet were bound. The broth of monkey bones was to soften her feet, to make them malleable enough to fit into the tiny pair of red satin boots that her mother had made for her and which now sat upon the altar like an offering to the gods.

'I have paid for the footbinder, and I shall have one!' snarled Lady Guo Guo, and followed by her maids, she lurched angrily from the temple.

The sunlight caught her unawares. It struck her like the projectile of a crossbow, and she was momentarily blinded and confused. She and her small procession immediately snapped open their fans, shielded their eyes from above and held this pose, unmoving, like an operatic tableau. Those in the courtyard pushed forward and back, chattering among themselves, eagerly awaiting instructions. The zither players struck up Lady Guo Guo's favourite tune, and as her eyes adjusted to the light, she dimly perceived members of the crowd being shoved to and fro and finally propelled to one side to permit the entrance of, she focused her eyes sharply to make sure, her husband and master, the prefect, Lord Guo Guo.

Lady Guo Guo bowed as did the entire crowd and said, 'Welcome, my lord, an unexpected pleasure. I had no idea you were in the neighbourhood. You are stopping at The Five Enjoyments Tea House, I presume?'

'Ah, if only I could afford to,' he replied pointedly. 'But alas, I'm just passing through on a visit to the sub-prefect.'

'Let us climb the belvedere,' began Lady Guo Guo nervously, 'for there we can speak in private.' She hurried toward the turret, which was hard by the temple. 'I call it Hereafter-View, for its beauty is quite suffocating.' Lord Guo Guo followed and then stopped, carefully examining the stones at the belvedere's base.

'What stone is this?' he asked. His copyist followed, taking notes.

'Marble,' Lady Guo Guo answered nonchalantly as if he ought to know.

'From?'

'From . . .' Lady Guo Guo concentrated intently. 'From from, from – forgive me, husband, I have forgotten the name. I am overwrought. Your arrival has coincided with Pleasure Mouse's footbinding. The propitious hour is upon us; I cannot –'

'Perhaps I can help you remember. It is a Chinese name?'

'No,' snapped the Lady, and fled into the belvedere and up the winding marble steps. The Lord followed.

'No? Not a Chinese name, then presumably not from China. Imported then. Let me think. Annam? Champa?'

Lady Guo Guo disappeared beyond the next turn in the stairs. The Lord stayed behind.

'What?' he cried out. 'Not even from the East? How luxurious! From the West, then. Ah, I know! Egypt!' Lord Guo Guo removed a knife from his sash and proceeded to carve a message into the marble wall. The knife scraped unpleasantly against the stone, and curious as to the noise, Lady Guo Guo reappeared around the bend. The message read: 'Paid for by the prefect, Lord Guo Guo,' and the date,

'1260'. The Lady gasped. 'How dare you deface my belvedere?' she demanded.

'How dare you use my wealth to make the merchants rich? Pretty soon there will be no aristocracy left. At the rate you are spending, I shall be the first to go.' Lord Guo Guo put away his knife.

'If you are so fearful, why do you not impose excessive taxes or put a ceiling on prices as you did last year when you bought yourself your title? As it is, I must purchase everything from the shops you own under a fraudulent name, and shoddy merchandise it is too! This marble was my one extravagance –'

'No more credit,' Lord Guo Guo said simply, and Lady Guo Guo sank to her knees and sobbed.

'You men are so cruel,' she cried, her tears dropping to the marble step. 'Building this tomb is my one last pleasure, and you will take it from me just as you took from me my ability to walk. Well, let me tell you, you may cripple me in this endeavour, but you will never stop me.'

'Men took from you your ability to walk?' the Lord said incredulously. 'Is it the man who pulls the binding cloth to cripple a daughter's feet? No man could do a thing like that. No man could bear it.'

'No man would marry a natural-footed woman. There is more to binding feet than just the binding!'

'If all women were natural-footed, a man would have no choice,' Lord Guo Guo concluded and began descending the stairs.

Lady Guo Guo shook with fury and called after him. 'Shall I leave your daughter natural-footed then? Yes. Yes. You are quite right and logical. Let our family be the one to begin the new fashion, and we shall begin it with the perky Pleasure Mouse!' In her anger, the Lady called out theatrically to her maid, 'Wild Mint! Tell the footbinder to go away; we shall not need her.'

'The footbinder?' asked Lord Guo Guo quietly. 'Then you will not do the binding yourself?'

'Shall the prefect Lord Guo Guo's daughter be natural-footed? Your choice, my lord.'

'So.' The Lord grinned. 'You've hired another to do the job for you? An interesting twist.'

'Natural feet or lotus hooks? Be quick, my husband, the propitious hour is passing and will not come again for a full twelve seasons of growth.'

Lord Guo Guo grew impatient at this last remark and turned his back. 'These are women's things, your affairs, wife, not mine,' he muttered sullenly.

Lady Guo Guo tapped her tiny foot. 'What if I were to fall ill, creating a disturbance, right this moment and allow the propitious hour to pass?'

'I wouldn't let you,' Lord Guo Guo snarled.

'You could not prevent me. It is a women's ritual, my husband, and as such, depends on the good omen. A mother's falling ill during a ceremony at which no man can show his face, even a father, especially a father –'

'Would you harm your daughter to harm me? What is it you seek, wife?'

'Unlimited credit, sir. Decide quickly; there is little time left.'

Lord Guo Guo's nostrils flared. 'You have it, ma'am' were the words that he spat out as, robes flying, he hurtled through the belvedere door. Lady Guo Guo smiled to herself and followed quickly behind.

'Here, wife.' The Lord spoke through gritted teeth and thrust a walking stick into the Lady's arms. 'An ebony cane. Also imported like your marble from Africa. For the Pleasure Mouse, for after.'

'Thank you, my lord,' said Lady Guo Guo, bowing low, 'and a good journey, sir. Please come again.' And with that she was off, hobbling swiftly toward the temple courtyard before Wild Mint could send the footbinder away.

Pleasure Mouse looked around nervously at Lao Bing and the geomancer, who were whispering together.

'Well,' sniffed Lao Bing, 'if it comes to it, I'll do it myself then. I bound three daughters of my own with perfect success. Autumn Surprise won the Emperor's commendation for the most beauteous hooks at the Hu Street small foot contest. Now she's his concubine-in-waiting, if you don't mind.'

'Exquisite,' said the geomancer in his whiny voice. 'But did you hear about the Sung sisters?'

'What?'

'Rivals for the same young man, Black Mist cut up all of Blue Jade's tiny shoes and heaped them in the courtyard for all to see!'

'No!'

'Yes. And speaking of concubines-in-waiting, I hear the Emperor often keeps them waiting for years, and in the harems with only each other for company, I hear they use each other's hooks for –'

'The footbinder has arrived,' announced Lady Guo Guo as she entered the chamber. 'Let us begin.'

Lao Bing sent the geomancer a parting glance of daggers. 'Leave us,' she hissed and then turned to inspect the famous footbinder.

'Forgive me, everyone,' the footbinder waved heartily at those assembled as she strode into the temple. 'The youngest daughter of the Wang family persists in unbinding on the sly. Each time she does this I tell her I shall only have to pull the bindings tighter. After all, we have two reputations to think of, hers and mine. But you can't tell a child about Lotus Boats, as you all know. They never believe it can happen to them.'

Lao Bing, Lady Guo Guo, and the various maidservants in the chamber nodded in understanding.

'Children think we are born with small feet,' began Lao Bing.

'Oh, if only we were,' sighed Lady Guo Guo, interrupting.

Lao Bing continued. 'But once in Shensi Province, I saw a natural-footed peasant girl, well, you talk of Lotus Boats, but really Fox Paws would be more accurate. Feet as large as a catapult repairman's.'

Pleasure Mouse twisted around and stared at the footbinder. Barely four feet high and as round as a carved ivory ball, the tiny woman removed her pointy-hooded homespun cloak and revealed herself to be a Buddhist nun. Shaved head and eyebrows, saffron robes, face unadorned by powder or blush, the little fat turnip of a woman bent down and picked up her basket and hurried toward the altar.

Lao Bing gasped in horror and took Lady Guo Guo roughly to one side. 'What is the meaning of this? She's not wearing shoes! She's barefooted and natural-footed. I've never been so embarrassed, and what about Pleasure Mouse? I –'

'Shh!' Lady Guo Guo took Lao Bing's hands and tried to

explain. 'Not having bound feet herself, she is better able to make a really good job of binding others. It is an aesthetic act to her, objective, don't you see? For us it is so much more, so clouded. Our sympathy overcomes our good judgment. Pleasure Mouse's feet will be as hummingbirds, you'll see.'

'All right,' sniffed Lao Bing. 'I suppose it make some sense. But my aunt did my bindings, and merciless she was.' Lao Bing's voice had risen as she remembered. 'I have always felt that had it been my own mama, some sympathy might have been shown for my agony.'

'Perhaps,' called the footbinder from across the room. 'Perhaps not.'

'At any rate,' Lao Bing, outraged at the interruption, went on, 'I blame such newfangled notions on the barbarians from the North, the Mongol hordes. I pray such contaminate influences do not sully my perky Pleasure Mouse. But if they do, I personally –'

'Silence, please,' boomed the footbinder. And then, 'Send away the throngs outside the temple!'

'No kiteflyer?' asked Lady Guo Guo timidly. 'But we have always had a kiteflyer for before. It is the last time –'

'No. No. The feet swell from the running and it is far too difficult. As for the teller of obscene stories, he was present when I bound the Wang girls and, sadly, he is simply neither obscene nor funny.'

'He seemed amply disgusting to me,' mused Lady Guo Guo as she padded toward the chamber door.

'Yes, foul,' agreed Lao Bing.

'Wild Mint.' Lady Guo Guo's number one maidservant rushed forward and curtsied. 'Clear the courtyard.'

'But the man with the performing fish?'

'Keep him on retainer. Perhaps for the inaugural ceremonies.'

Wild Mint nodded and rushed out. Some angry murmurs rose and fell, but soon there was bright, hot quiet outside, disturbed now and then only by the buzz of insects. Wild Mint re-entered the chamber and took up her post behind a red-lacquered pillar.

'Where is Tiger Mouse?' Lao Bing was whispering to Lady Guo Guo.

'I am afraid she is still too delicate to attend the ritual. She cannot as yet see the humour in it.' Lady Guo Guo placed her finger across her lips to command silence then and turned her attention to what the footbinder was doing.

'What are you doing?' Pleasure Mouse was asking.

The footbinder trained her beady eyes on the child and answered directly, 'I am tying you to the chair with leather thongs.' She finished securing the last arm and leg and paused to examine her handiwork.

'Why?' asked Pleasure Mouse, pulling a bit against the bonds.

'It hurts, Pleasure Mouse, and if you writhe all over the place you will interfere with perfection of the binding. Now here, grasp these water chestnuts in each hand and when it hurts, squeeze them with all your might and if you are lucky, your feet will turn out no bigger than they are.'

Please Mouse took the water chestnuts and squeezed them in her palms. The footbinder scurried around in front of the altar, head bent to her task and mumbling to herself.

'Here's a handkerchief to wipe the tears. Here's my knife. The binding cloth. Alum. Red jasmine powder. All right. I think we are all ready. Is it the propitious hour?' The footbinder glanced at Lady Guo Guo, who nodded and came forward to one side of Pleasure Mouse's chair. She patted the little girl on the shoulder and smiled weakly. Lao Bing came forward as well and stood on the opposite side. 'If we begin just at the propitious hour, it won't hurt,' the old lady said without much conviction.

Warm Milk entered at this moment by the side door of the temple and sat without comment next to Lao Bing on a stool carried in by her maidservants. Warm Milk did not look well, so swollen was she with womanly waters pressurized by the heat. But she smiled at Pleasure Mouse and waved one of her long, long sleeves.

The footbinder took up the knife and knelt down in front of the chair and concentrated on the broth of monkey bones and Pleasure Mouse's feet. She draped a towel over her knees and picked up one foot and dried it. She then took the knife and brought it toward Pleasure Mouse's toes. The little girl shrieked with terror and fought against her bonds. Her mother and her aunt held her down and tried to placate her. Warm Milk stood up hurriedly and cried out.

'Do not be afraid, Pleasure Mouse. She means only to cut your toenails. Truly, little one, truly.'

Pleasure Mouse relaxed and tears ran down her face and on to the new silk robe that her mother had embroidered just for this occasion. The footbinder grabbed Pleasure Mouse's handkerchief, dabbed her cheeks and proceeded to cut her toenails.

'Now, what are the rules that all ladies must obey? Let me hear them while I cut.'

Pleasure Mouse recited in a clear, sad voice:

> 'Do not walk with toes pointed upwards.
> Do not stand with heels in mid-air.
> Do not move skirt when sitting.
> Do not move feet when lying down.
> Do not remove the binding, for there is nothing aesthetic beneath it.'

'And because, once bound, a foot does not feel well unbound. Excellent, Pleasure Mouse,' said the footbinder setting down her knife and rubbing the child's feet with alum. 'I can see that once your hooks are formed, you will be quite a little temptress.' The footbinder winked lewdly at Lao Bing and Lady Guo Guo. 'I predict buttocks like giant pitted plums, thighs like sacks of uncombed wool, a vagina with more folds than a go-between's message, and a nature as subdued as a eunuch's desire.'

The women in the temple tittered modestly, and Pleasure Mouse blushed and squirmed beneath the bonds.

Suddenly, Pleasure Mouse became mesmerized by a beauteous ring on the right index finger of the footbinder's dimpled hand. It flashed in the light of the prayer candles, and as the footbinder laid out the silk binding cloths, it created, in mid-air, a miniature fireworks display.

'What a splendid ring,' murmured Pleasure Mouse.

'What ring, dear?' asked Lady Guo Guo.

'That one, there –' Pleasure Mouse indicated the footbinder's right hand with a bob of her head, but the ring had gone, vanished.

'Never mind,' said Pleasure Mouse, and squeezed the chestnuts in her tiny hands.

The footbinder took hold of the child's right foot and,

leaving the big toe free, bent the other toes beneath the foot and bound them down with the long, silk cloth. The women gathered around the chair and watched the process intently. She then took a second cloth and bound, as tightly as she could, around the heel of the foot and down, again over and around the now bent toes, with the result that the heel and the toes were brought as close together as they could go, and the arch of the foot was forced upward in the knowledge that eventually it would break, restructure itself and foreshorten the foot. The last binding was applied beneath the big toe and around the heel, pushing the appendage up and inward like the point of a moon sickle. When the right foot was done, the footbinder bound the left foot in the same manner, removed the basin of monkey-bone broth and retrieved the tiny shoes from the altar. She knelt before the Pleasure Mouse and, as she forced her bound feet into the shoes, Lady Guo Guo intoned a prayer: 'Oh, venerable ancestors, smile favourably upon my perky Pleasure Mouse, that she may marry well and one day see her own daughter's entry into womanhood. Take the first step, my child. Take the first step.'

Lady Guo Guo, Lao Bing and the footbinder untied the leather thongs and released Pleasure Mouse's arms and legs. Pleasure Mouse was silent and rigid in the chair.

'Up, dear,' said Lao Bing, taking the child's elbow. 'Up, you must walk.'

'Take the first step,' said Lady Guo Guo, grasping the other elbow.

'Up, child,' said the footbinder, and she stood Pleasure Mouse on her newly fashioned feet.

Pleasure Mouse screamed. She looked down at the tiny shoes on her now strangely shaped feet and she screamed again. She jerked toward her mother and screamed a third time and tried to throw herself to the ground. The women held her up. 'Walk,' they chanted all together, 'you must walk or you will sicken. The pain goes away in time.'

'In about two years' time,' crooned the courtesan, Honey Tongue. She had suddenly appeared in place of the footbinder who seemed to have vanished.

'Walk, little one, no matter how painful,' Lao Bing grabbed the flailing child and shook her by the shoulders. 'We have all been through it, can't you see that? You must trust us. Now walk!'

The women stepped back, and Pleasure Mouse hobbled two or three steps. Waves of agony as sharp as stiletto blades traversed the six-year-old's legs and thighs, her spine and head. She bent over like an aged crone and staggered around, not fully comprehending why she was being forced to crush her own toes with her own body weight.

Pleasure Mouse lunged toward the apparition and fell on the altar, sobbing and coughing. Honey Tongue enveloped her in a warm and perfumed aura.

'Do you wish to stay on earth, or do you wish to come with me?' Honey Tongue waved her long, long sleeve, and for a moment all was still. The women froze in their positions. Time was suspended in the temple.

'You can be a constellation, a profusion of stars in the summer sky, a High Lama in the great mountains to the East – a man, but holy. Or an orchid in the Perfect Afterlife Garden. Or you may stay as you are. It is your choice, Pleasure Mouse.'

The little girl thought for a long while and then answered, 'The only way to escape one's destiny is to enjoy it. I will stay here.'

Honey Tongue vanished, and in her place reappeared the small, fat cabbage of a footbinder. The women wept and chattered, Pleasure Mouse moaned and bellowed in agony, and Time, its feet unbound, bounded on.

'Come, Pleasure Mouse. Sit,' said the footbinder, and with her strong, muscled arms, she lifted the little girl and set her in the chair before the altar. The child sighed with relief and hung her head. The tiny shoes were stained with blood, as were her dreams of ladyhood. She whimpered softly. Warm Milk lurched painfully to her side, bent down and began to massage Pleasure Mouse's small burning legs. The women gathered around the altar, and the footbinder lit two prayer strips and recited:

'Oh, Little Footed Miss, Goddess of our female fate, keep the Pleasure Mouse healthy and safe. Let her hooks be as round, white dumplings. Let them not turn to dead, brown shreds at the end of her legs. Let her blood not be poisoned or her spirit. Let her learn to walk daintily without pain, and let her not envy those who can run for they are lowly and abused. Ay, let her never forget: for them, running is not luxury but necessity. Let her marry a relative of the Emperor, if not the Emperor himself. And let her have many sons that, when the season comes, she might enter the afterlife like a princess.'

Lady Guo Guo snapped her fingers. 'Wild Mint, escort our new lady back to her chambers, if you please. I will come later, Pleasure Mouse, when the sun goes down, and I will bring with me an ebony cane sent by your father from the city. Look, little one, here is Spring Rain. Wild Mint sent for her that she might see you in your ladylike mantle.'

'My word,' gasped Lao Bing, 'the doll wears the tiny shoes!'

Lady Guo Guo laughed. 'So she does. How odd. Perhaps Tiger Mouse –'

Pleasure Mouse grabbed Spring Rain and ripped the shoes off her feet. She clasped the rag doll to her chest and stumbled from the temple.

Lady Guo Guo took the footbinder aside and paid her. The women wandered aimlessly from the temple into the sunlight.

'Oh dear,' sighed Lao Bing. 'I hurt all over again. As if fifty years ago were yesterday.' She shielded her eyes from the sun with her fan.

'Must it always be so violent?' murmured Warm Milk.

'I don't know if it must be, but it always is,' said the footbinder as she and Lady Guo Guo emerged from the temple.

'Have many young girls . . . died?' asked Lady Guo Guo.

'Some prefer death, Lady Gee, it is the way of the world.' The footbinder climbed into her sedan chair. 'I must be off,' she said. 'Keep the child on her hooks. I shall return in one week to wash and rebind. Please have the next smallest pair of shoes ready for my return. Goodbye.'

Warm Milk curtsied to Lao Bing and Lady Guo Guo and with the aid of her maids, tottered past the departing procession toward her apartments.

Lao Bing and Lady Guo Guo watched the footbinder's sedan chair disappear through the Sun Gate, and when it was gone, Lao Bing clucked and said, 'A footbinder. A footbinder. Ah, the seasons do change. I feel old, Little Sister.

My toes are flattened out like cat tongues. The soles of my feet rise and fall like mountain peaks. How much did you pay her?'

'Thirty cash.'

'Thirty cash!'

'It was worth it not to be the cause of pain,' Lady Guo Guo said simply.

'Ah, yes, I see,' sighed Lao Bing. 'Well then, perhaps she won't blame you although –'

'After Tiger Mouse, I could not bear – you understand?'

'Of course.' Lao Bing patted her brother's wife on the shoulder and, with a nod of her head, summoned her sedan chair.

'Farewell, Little Sister. We shall meet again in the city. I shall regale the lord, your husband, with tales of the magnificence of your burial tomb, but be frugal, child, his patience falters.'

'Thank you for your counsel, Lao Bing. It is well taken.'

Lady Guo Guo closed the door of the sedan chair and waited until the pole bearers hoisted up the old lady and trotted away down the temple path.

The sun was iron-hot and glaring. Lady Guo Guo swept into a shadow of the temple eaves and stood there by herself, staring into nothingness, occasionally and absentmindedly waving her fan. After a time she ventured out into the sunlight, determined to make her way to the Pavilion of Coolness, where, she had decided, today she would take her rest. She padded past the Hereafter-View belvedere, across the Courtyard of a Thousand Fools, and right in front of the Zither Players' Wing, where the zither players caught sight of her and at once struck up her favourite tune. 'China Nights' was the name of the song, and she waited politely in the white-hot sunlight until the final pings had died away. After bowing in thanks, she continued on, slower now, as she was losing strength. By the time she reached the Pavilion of Coolness, her hooks were puffy and throbbing like beating hearts.

The Kiss

Angela Carter

The winters in Central Asia are piercing and bleak, while the sweating, foetid summers bring cholera, dysentery and mosquitoes, but, in April, the air caresses like the touch of the inner skin of the thigh and the scent of all the flowering trees douses this city's throat-catching whiff of cesspits.

Every city has its own internal logic. Imagine a city drawn in straightforward, geometric shapes with crayons from a child's colouring box, in ochre, in white, in pale terracotta. Low, blonde terraces of houses seem to rise out of the whitish, pinkish earth as if born from it, not built out of it. There is a faint, gritty dust over everything, like the dust those pastel crayons leave on your fingers.

Against these bleached pallors, the irridescent crusts of ceramic tiles that cover the ancient mausoleums ensorcellate the eye. The throbbing blue of Islam transforms itself to green while you look at it. Beneath a bulbous dome alternately lapis lazuli and veridian, the bones of Tamburlaine, the scourge of Asia, lie in a jade tomb. We are visiting an authentically fabulous city. We are in Samarkand.

The Revolution promised the Uzbek peasant women clothes of silk and on this promise, at least, did not welch. They wear tunics of flimsy satin, pink and yellow, red and white, black and white, red, green and white, in blotched stripes of brilliant colours that dazzle like an optical illusion, and they bedeck themselves with much jewellery made of red glass.

They always seem to be frowning because they paint a thick, black line straight across their foreheads that takes their eyebrows from one side of their faces to the other without a break. They rim their eyes with kohl. They look startling. They fasten their long hair in two or three dozen whirling plaits. Young girls wear little velvet caps embroidered with metallic thread and beadwork. Older women cover their heads with a couple of scarves of flower-printed wool, one bound tight over the forehead, the other hanging loosely on to the shoulders. Nobody has worn a veil for sixty years.

They walk as purposefully as if they did not live in an imaginary city. They do not know that they themselves and their turbaned, sheepskin jacketed, booted menfolk are creatures as extraordinary to the foreign eye as a unicorn. They exist, in all their glittering and innocent exoticism, in direct contradiction to history. They do not know what I know about them. They do not know that this city is not the entire world. All they know of the world is this city, beautiful as an illusion, where irises grow in the gutters. In the tea-house a green parrot nudges the bars of its wicker cage.

The market has a sharp, green smell. A girl with black-barred brows sprinkles water from a glass over radishes. In this early part of the year, you can buy only last summer's dried fruit – apricots, peaches, raisins – except for a few, precious, wrinkled pomegranates, stored in sawdust through the winter and now split open on the stall to show how a wet nest of garnets remains within. A local speciality of Samarkand is salted apricot kernels, more delicious, even, than pistachios.

An old woman sells arum lilies. This morning, she came from the mountains, where wild tulips have put out flowers like blown bubbles of blood, and the wheedling turtle-doves are nesting among the rocks. This old woman dips bread into a cup of buttermilk for her lunch and eats slowly. When she has sold her lilies, she will go back to the place where they are growing.

She scarcely seems to inhabit time. Or, it is as if she were waiting for Scheherezade to perceive a final dawn had come and, the last tale of all concluded, fall silent. Then, the lily-seller might vanish.

A goat is nibbling wild jasmine among the ruins of the mosque that was built by the beautiful wife of Tamburlaine.

Tamburlaine's wife started to build this mosque for him as a surprise, while he was away at the wars, but when she got word of his imminent return, one arch still remained unfinished. She went directly to the architect and begged him to hurry but the architect told her that he would complete the work in time only if she gave him a kiss. One kiss, one single kiss.

Tamburlaine's wife was not only very beautiful and very virtuous but also very clever. She went to the market, bought a basket of eggs, boiled them hard and stained them a dozen different colours. She called the architect to the palace, showed him the basket and told him to choose any egg he liked and eat it. He took a red egg. What does it taste like? Like an egg. Eat another.

He took a green egg.

What does *that* taste like? Like the red egg. Try again.

He ate a purple egg.

One egg tastes just the same as any other egg, if they are fresh, he said.

There you are! she said. Each of these eggs looks different to the rest but they all taste the same. So you may kiss any one of my serving women that you like but you must leave me alone.

Very well, said the architect. But soon he came back to her and this time he was carrying a tray with three bowls on it, and you would have thought the bowls were all full of water.

Drink from each of these bowls, he said.

She took a drink from the first bowl, then from the second; but how she coughed and spluttered when she took a mouthful from the third bowl, because it contained, not water, but vodka.

This vodka and that water both look alike but each tastes quite different, he said. And it is the same with love.

Then Tamburlaine's wife kissed the architect on the mouth. He went back to the mosque and finished the arch the same day that victorious Tamburlaine rode into Samarkand with his army and banners and his cages full of captive kings. But when Tamburlaine went to visit his wife, she turned away from him because no woman will return to the harem after she has tasted vodka. Tamburlaine beat her with a knout until she told him she had kissed the architect and then he sent his executioners hotfoot to the mosque.

The executioners saw the architect standing on top of the arch and ran up the stairs with their knives drawn but when he heard them coming he grew wings and flew away to Persia.

This is a story in simple, geometric shapes and the bold colours of a child's box of crayons. This Tamburlaine's wife of the story would have painted a black stripe laterally across her forehead and done up her hair in a dozen, dozen tiny plaits, like any other Uzbek woman. She would have bought red and white radishes from the market for her husband's dinner. After she ran away from him perhaps she made her living in the market. Perhaps she sold lilies there.

To Hell with Dying

Alice Walker

'To hell with dying,' my father would say. 'These children want Mr Sweet!'

Mr Sweet was a diabetic and an alcoholic and a guitar player and lived down the road from us on a neglected cotton farm. My older brothers and sisters got the most benefit from Mr Sweet, for when they were growing up he had quite a few years ahead of him and so was capable of being called back from the brink of death any number of times – whenever the voice of my father reached him as he lay expiring. 'To hell with dying, man,' my father would say, pushing the wife away from the bedside (in tears although she knew the death was not necessarily the last one unless Mr Sweet really wanted it to be). 'These children want Mr Sweet!' And they did want him, for at a signal from Father they would come crowding around the bed and throw themselves on the covers, and whoever was the smallest at the time would kiss him all over his wrinkled brown face and begin to tickle him so that he would laugh all down in his stomach, and his moustache, which was long and sort of straggly, would shake like Spanish moss and was also that color.

Mr Sweet had been ambitious as a boy, wanted to be a doctor or lawyer or sailor, only to find that black men fare better if they are not. Since he could become none of these things he turned to fishing as his only earnest career and playing the guitar as his only claim to doing anything extraordinarily well. His son, the only one that he and his wife, Miss Mary, had, was shiftless as the day is long and spent money as if he were trying to see the bottom of the mint, which Mr Sweet would tell him was the clean brown palm of his hand. Miss Mary loved her 'baby,' however, and worked hard to get him the 'lil'l necessaries' of life, which turned out mostly to be women.

Mr Sweet was a tall, thinnish man with thick kinky hair going dead white. He was dark brown, his eyes were very squinty and sort of bluish, and he chewed Brown Mule tobacco. He was constantly on the verge of being blind drunk, for he brewed his own liquor and was not in the least a stingy sort of man, and was always very melancholy and sad, though frequently when he was 'feelin' good' he'd dance around the yard with us, usually keeling over just as my mother came to see what the commotion was.

Toward all of us children he was very kind, and had the grace to be shy with us, which is unusual in grown-ups. He had great respect for my mother for she never held his drunkenness against him and would let us play with him even when he was about to fall in the fireplace from drink. Although Mr Sweet would sometimes lose complete or nearly complete control of his head and neck so that he would loll in his chair, his mind remained strangely acute and his speech not too affected. His ability to be drunk and sober at the same time made him an ideal playmate, for he was as weak as we were and we could usually best him in wrestling, all the while keeping a fairly coherent conversation going.

We never felt anything of Mr Sweet's age when we played with him. We loved his wrinkles and would draw some on our brows to be like him, and his white hair was my special treasure and he knew it and would never come to visit us just after he had had his hair cut off at the barbershop. Once he came to our house for something, probably to see my father about fertilizer for his crops because, although he never paid the slightest attention to his crops, he liked to know what things would be best to use on them if he ever did. Anyhow, he had not come with his hair since he had just had it shaved off at the barbershop. He wore a huge straw hat to keep off the sun and also to keep his head away from me. But as soon as I saw him I ran up and demanded that he take me up and kiss me with his funny beard which smelled so strongly of tobacco. Looking forward to burying my small fingers into his woolly hair I threw away his hat only to find he had done something to his hair, that it was no longer there! I let out a squall which made my mother think that Mr Sweet had finally dropped me in the well or something and from that day I've been wary of men in hats. However, not long after, Mr Sweet showed up with his hair grown out and just as white and kinky and impenetrable as it ever was.

Mr Sweet used to call me his princess, and I believed it. He made me feel pretty at five and six, and simply outrageously devastating at the blazing age of eight and a half. When he came to our house with his guitar the whole family would stop whatever they were doing to sit around him and listen to him play. He liked to play 'Sweet Georgia Brown,' that was what he called me sometimes, and also he liked to play 'Caldonia' and all sorts of sweet, sad, wonderful songs which he sometimes made up. It was from one of these songs that I learned that he had had to marry Miss Mary when he had in fact loved somebody else (now living in Chica-go, or De-stroy, Michigan). He was not sure that Joe Lee, her 'baby,' was also his baby. Sometimes he would cry and that was an indication that he was about to die again. And so we would all get prepared, for we were sure to be called upon.

I was seven the first time I remember actually participating in one of Mr Sweet's 'revivals' – my parents told me I had participated before, I had been the one chosen to kiss him and tickle him long before I knew the rite of Mr Sweet's rehabilitation. He had come to our house, it was a few years after his wife's death, and was very sad, and also, typically, very drunk. He sat on the floor next to me and my older brother, the rest of the children were grown up and lived elsewhere, and began to play his guitar and cry. I held his woolly head in my arms and wished I could have been old enough to have been the woman he loved so much and that I had not been lost years and years ago.

When he was leaving, my mother said to us that we'd better sleep light that night for we'd probably have to go over to Mr Sweet's before daylight. And we did. For soon after we had gone to bed one of the neighbors knocked on our door and called my father and said that Mr Sweet was sinking fast and if he wanted to get in a word before the crossover he'd better shake a leg and get over to Mr Sweet's house. All the neighbors knew to come to our house if something was wrong with Mr Sweet, but they did not know how we always managed to make him well, or at least stop him from dying, when he was often so near death. As soon as we heard the cry we got up, my brother and I and my mother and father, and put on our clothes. We hurried out of the house and down the road for we were always afraid that we might someday be too late and Mr Sweet would get tired of dallying.

When we got to the house, a very poor shack really, we found the front room full of neighbors and relatives and someone met us at the door and said that it was all very sad that old Mr Sweet Little (for Little was his family name, although we mostly ignored it) was about to kick the bucket. My parents were advised not to take my brother and me into the 'death room,' seeing we were so young and all, but we were so much more accustomed to the death room than he that we ignored him and dashed in without giving his warning a second thought. I was almost in tears, for these deaths upset me fearfully, and the thought of how much depended on me and my brother (who was such a ham most of the time) made me very nervous.

The doctor was bending over the bed and turned back to tell us for at least the tenth time in the history of my family that, alas, old Mr Sweet Little was dying and that the children had best not see the face of implacable death (I didn't know what 'implacable' was, but whatever it was, Mr Sweet was not!). My father pushed him rather abruptly out of the way saying, as he always did and very loudly for he was saying it to Mr Sweet, 'To hell with dying, man, these children want Mr Sweet' – which was my cue to throw myself upon the bed and kiss Mr Sweet all around the whiskers and under the eyes and around the collar of his nightshirt where he smelled so strongly of all sorts of things, mostly liniment.

I was very good at bringing him around, for as soon as I saw that he was struggling to open his eyes I knew he was going to be all right, and so could finish my revival sure of success. As soon as his eyes were open he would begin to smile and that way I knew that I had surely won. Once, though, I got a tremendous scare, for he could not open his eyes and later I learned that he had had a stroke and that one side of his face was stiff and hard to get into motion. When he began to smile I could tickle him in earnest because I was sure that nothing would get in the way of his laughter, although once he began to cough so hard that he almost threw me off his stomach, but that was when I was very small, little more than a baby, and my bushy hair had gotten in his nose.

When we were sure he would listen to us we would ask him why he was in bed and when he was coming to see us again and could we play with his guitar, which more than likely would be leaning against the bed. His eyes would get all misty and he would sometimes cry out loud, but we never let it embarrass us, for he knew that we loved him and that we sometimes cried too for no reason. My parents would leave the room to just the three of us; Mr Sweet, by that time, would be propped up in bed with a number of pillows behind his head and with me sitting and lying on his shoulder and along his chest. Even when he had trouble breathing he would not ask me to get down. Looking into my eyes he would shake his white head and run a scratchy old finger all around my hairline, which was rather low down, nearly to my eyebrows, and made some people say I looked like a baby monkey.

My brother was very generous in all this, he let me do all the revivaling – he had done it for years before I was born and so was glad to be able to pass it on to someone new. What he would do while I talked to Mr Sweet was pretend to play the guitar, in fact pretend that he was a young version of Mr Sweet, and it always made Mr Sweet glad to think that someone wanted to be like him – of course, we did not know this then, we played the thing by ear, and whatever he seemed to like, we did. We were desperately afraid that he was just going to take off one day and leave us.

It did not occur to us that we were doing anything special; we had not learned that death was final when it did come. We thought nothing of triumphing over it so many times, and in fact became a trifle contemptuous of people who let themselves be carried away. It did not occur to us that if our own father had been dying we could not have stopped it, that Mr Sweet was the only person over whom we had power.

When Mr Sweet was in his eighties I was studying in the

university many miles from home. I saw him whenever I went home, but he was never on the verge of dying that I could tell and I began to feel that my anxiety for his health and psychological well-being was unnecessary. By this time he not only had a moustache but a long flowing snow-white beard, which I loved and combed and braided for hours. He was very peaceful, fragile, gentle, and the only jarring note about him was his old steel guitar, which he still played in the old sad, sweet, down-home blues way.

On Mr Sweet's ninetieth birthday I was finishing my doctorate in Massachusetts and had been making arrangements to go home for several weeks' rest. That morning I got a telegram telling me that Mr Sweet was dying again and could I please drop everything and come home. Of course I could. My dissertation could wait and my teachers would understand when I explained to them when I got back. I ran to the phone, called the airport, and within four hours I was speeding along the dusty road to Mr Sweet's.

The house was more dilapidated than when I was last there, barely a shack, but it was overgrown with yellow roses which my family had planted many years ago. The air was heavy and sweet and very peaceful. I felt strange walking through the gate and up the old rickety steps. But the strangeness left me as I caught sight of the long white beard I loved so well flowing down the thin body over the familiar quilt coverlet. Mr Sweet!

His eyes were closed tight and his hands, crossed over his stomach, were thin and delicate, no longer scratchy. I remembered how always before I had run and jumped up on him just anywhere; now I knew he would not be able to support my weight. I looked around at my parents, and was surprised to see that my father and mother also looked old and frail. My father, his own hair very gray, leaned over the quietly sleeping old man, who, incidentally, smelled still of wine and tobacco, and said, as he'd done so many times, 'To hell with dying, man! My daughter is home to see Mr Sweet!' My brother had not been able to come as he was in the war in Asia. I bent down and gently stroked the closed eyes and gradually they began to open. The closed, wine-stained lips twitched a little, then parted in a warm, slightly embarrassed smile. Mr Sweet could see me and he recognized me and his eyes looked very spry and twinkly for a moment. I put my head down on the pillow next to his and we just looked at each other for a long time. Then he began to trace my peculiar hairline with a thin, smooth finger. I closed my eyes when his finger halted above my ear (he used to rejoice at the dirt in my ears when I was little), his hand stayed cupped around my cheek. When I opened my eyes, sure that I had reached him in time, his were closed.

Even at twenty-four how could I believe that I had failed? that Mr Sweet was really gone? He had never gone before. But when I looked up at my parents I saw that they were holding back tears. They had loved him dearly. He was like a piece of rare and delicate china which was always being saved from breaking and which finally fell. I looked long at the old face, the wrinkled forehead, the red lips, the hands that still reached out to me. Soon I felt my father pushing something cool into my hands. It was Mr Sweet's guitar. He had asked them months before to give it to me; he had known that even if I came next time he would not be able to respond in the old way. He did not want me to feel that my trip had been for nothing.

The old guitar! I plucked the strings, hummed 'Sweet Georgia Brown.' The magic of Mr Sweet lingered still in the cool steel box. Through the window I could catch the fragrant delicate scent of tender yellow roses. The man on the high old-fashioned bed with the quilt coverlet and the flowing white beard had been my first love.

Here We Are

Dorothy Parker

The young man in the new blue suit finished arranging the glistening luggage in tight corners of the Pullman compartment. The train had leaped at curves and bounced along straightaways, rendering balance a praiseworthy achievement and a sporadic one; and the young man had pushed and hoisted and tucked and shifted the bags with concentrated care.

Nevertheless, eight minutes for the settling of two suitcases and a hat-box is a long time.

He sat down, leaning back against bristled green plush, in the seat opposite the girl in beige. She looked as new as a peeled egg. Her hat, her fur, her frock, her gloves were glossy and stiff with novelty. On the arc of the thin, slippery sole of one beige shoe was gummed a tiny oblong of white paper, printed with the price set and paid for that slipper and its fellow, and the name of the shop that had dispensed them.

She had been staring raptly out of the window, drinking in the big weathered signboards that extolled the phenomena of codfish without bones and screens no rust could corrupt. As the young man sat down, she turned politely from the pane, met his eyes, started a smile and got it about half done, and rested her gaze just above his right shoulder.

'Well!' the young man said.

'Well!' she said.

'Well, here we are,' he said.

'Here we are,' she said. 'Aren't we?'

'I should say we were,' he said. 'Eeyop. Here we are.'

'Well!' she said.

'Well!' he said. 'Well. How does it feel to be an old married lady?'

'Oh, it's too soon to ask me that,' she said. 'At least – I mean. Well, I mean, goodness, we've only been married about three hours, haven't we?'

The young man studied his wrist-watch as if he were just acquiring the knack of reading time.

'We have been married,' he said, 'exactly two hours and twenty-six minutes.'

'My,' she said. 'It seems like longer.'

'No,' he said. 'It isn't hardly half-past six yet.'

'It seems like later,' she said. 'I guess it's because it starts getting dark so early.'

'It does, at that,' he said. 'The nights are going to be pretty long from now on. I mean. I mean – well, it starts getting dark early.'

'I didn't have any idea what time it was,' she said. 'Everything was so mixed up, I sort of don't know where I am, or what it's all about. Getting back from the church, and then all those people, and then changing all my clothes, and then everybody throwing things, and all. Goodness, I don't see how people do it every day.'

'Do what?' he said.

'Get married,' she said. 'When you think of all the people, all over the world, getting married just as if it was nothing. Chinese people and everybody. Just as if it wasn't anything.'

'Well, let's not worry about people all over the world,' he said. 'Let's don't think about a lot of Chinese. We've got something better to think about. I mean. I mean – well, what do we care about them?'

'I know,' she said. 'But I just sort of got to thinking of them, all of them, all over everywhere, doing it all the time. At least, I mean – getting married, you know. And it's – well, it's sort of such a big thing to do, it makes you feel queer. You think of them, all of them, all doing it just like it wasn't happening. And how does anybody know what's going to happen next?'

'Let them worry,' he said. 'We don't have to. We know darn well what's going to happen next. I mean. I mean – well, we know it's going to be great. Well, we know we're going to be happy. Don't we?'

'Oh, of course,' she said. 'Only you think of all the people, and you have to sort of keep thinking. It makes you feel funny. An awful lot of people that get married, it doesn't turn out so well. And I guess they all must have thought it was going to be great.'

'Come on, now,' he said. 'This is no way to start a honeymoon, with all this thinking going on. Look at us – all married and everything done. I mean. The wedding all done and all.'

'Ah, it was nice, wasn't it?' she said. 'Did you really like my veil?'

'You looked great,' he said. 'Just great.'

'Oh, I'm terribly glad,' she said. 'Ellie and Louise looked lovely, didn't they? I'm terribly glad they did finally decide on pink. They looked perfectly lovely.'

'Listen,' he said. 'I want to tell you something. When I was standing up there in that old church waiting for you to come up, and I saw those two bridesmaids, I thought to myself, I thought, "Well, I never knew Louise could look like that!" Why, she'd have knocked anybody's eye out.'

'Oh, really?' she said. 'Funny. Of course, everybody thought her dress and hat were lovely, but a lot of people seemed to think she looked sort of tired. People have been saying that a lot, lately. I tell them I think it's awfully mean of them going around saying that about her. I tell them they've got to remember that Louise isn't so terribly young any more, and they've got to expect her to look like that. Louise can say she's twenty-three all she wants to, but she's a good deal nearer twenty-seven.'

'Well, she was certainly a knock-out at the wedding,' he said. 'Boy!'

'I'm terribly glad you thought so,' she said. 'I'm glad someone did. How did you think Ellie looked?'

'Why, I honestly didn't get a look at her,' he said.

'Oh, really?' she said. 'Well, I certainly think that's too bad. I don't suppose I ought to say it about my own sister, but I never saw anybody look as beautiful as Ellie looked today. And always so sweet and unselfish, too. And you didn't even notice her. But you never pay attention to Ellie, anyway. Don't think I haven't noticed it. It makes me feel just terrible. It makes me feel just awful, that you don't like my own sister.'

'I do like her!' he said. 'I'm crazy for Ellie. I think she's a great kid.'

'Don't think it makes any difference to Ellie!' she said. 'Ellie's got enough people crazy about her. It isn't anything to her whether you like her or not. Don't flatter yourself she cares! Only, the only thing is, it makes it awfully hard for me you don't like her, that's the only thing. I keep thinking, when we come back and get in that apartment and everything, it's going to be awfully hard for me that you won't want my own sister to come and see me. It's going to make it awfully hard for me that you won't ever want my family around. I know how you feel about my family. Don't think I haven't seen it. Only, if you don't ever want to see them, that's your loss. Not theirs. Don't flatter yourself!'

'Oh, now, come on!' he said. 'What's all this talk about not wanting your family around? Why, you know how I feel about your family. I think your old lady – I think your mother's swell. And Ellie. And your father. What's all this talk?'

'Well, I've seen it,' she said. 'Don't think I haven't. Lots of people they get married, and they think it's going to be great and everything, and then it all goes to pieces because people don't like people's families, or something like that. Don't tell me! I've seen it happen.'

'Honey,' he said, 'what is all this? What are you getting all angry about? Hey, look, this is our honeymoon. What are you trying to start a fight for? Ah, I guess you're just feeling sort of nervous.'

'Me?' she said. 'What have I got to be nervous about? I mean. I mean, goodness, I'm not nervous.'

'You know, lots of times,' he said, 'they say that girls get kind of nervous and yippy on account of thinking about – I mean. I mean – well, it's like you said, things are all so sort of mixed up and everything, right now. But afterwards, it'll be all right. I mean. I mean – well, look, honey, you don't look any too comfortable. Don't you want to take your hat off? And let's don't ever fight, ever. Will we?'

'Ah, I'm sorry I was cross,' she said. 'I guess I did feel a little bit funny. All mixed up, and then thinking of all those people all over everywhere, and then being sort of 'way off here, all alone with you. It's so sort of different. It's sort of such a big thing. You can't blame a person for thinking, can you? Yes, don't let's ever, ever fight. We won't be like a whole lot of them. We won't fight or be nasty or anything. Will we?'

'You bet your life we won't,' he said.

'I guess I will take this darned old hat off,' she said. 'It kind of presses. Just put it up on the rack, will you, dear? Do you like it, sweetheart?'

'Looks good on you,' he said.

'No, but I mean,' she said, 'do you really like it?'

'Well, I'll tell you,' he said. 'I know this is the new style and everything like that, and it's probably great. I don't know anything about things like that. Only I like the kind of a hat like that blue hat you had. Gee, I liked that hat.'

'Oh, really?' she said. 'Well, that's nice. That's lovely. The first thing you say to me, as soon as you get me off on a train away from my family and everything, is that you don't like my hat. The first thing you say to your wife is you think she has terrible taste in hats. That's nice, isn't it?'

'Now, honey,' he said, 'I never said anything like that. I only said –'

'What you don't seem to realize,' she said, 'is this hat cost twenty-two dollars. Twenty-two dollars. And that horrible old blue thing you think you're so crazy about, that cost three ninety-five.'

'I don't give a darn what they cost,' he said. 'I only said – I said I liked that blue hat. I don't know anything about hats. I'll be crazy about this one as soon as I get used to it. Only it's kind of not like your other hats. I don't know about the new styles. What do I know about women's hats?'

'It's too bad,' she said, 'you didn't marry somebody that would get the kind of hats you'd like. Hats that cost three ninety-five. Why didn't you marry Louise? You always think she looks so beautiful. You'd love her taste in hats. Why didn't you marry her?'

'Ah, now, honey,' he said. 'For heaven's sakes!'

'Why didn't you marry her?' she said. 'All you've done, ever since we got on this train, is talk about her. Here I've sat and sat, and just listened to you saying how wonderful Louise is. I suppose that's nice, getting me all off here alone with you, and then raving about Louise right in front of my face. Why didn't you ask her to marry you? I'm sure she would have jumped at the chance. There aren't so many people asking her to marry them. It's too bad you didn't marry her. I'm sure you'd have been much happier.'

'Listen, baby,' he said, 'while you're talking about things like that, why didn't you marry Joe Brooks? I suppose he could have given you all the twenty-two-dollar hats you wanted, I suppose!'

'Well, I'm not so sure I'm not sorry I didn't,' she said. 'There! Joe Brooks wouldn't have waited until he got me all off alone and then sneered at my taste in clothes. Joe Brooks wouldn't ever hurt my feelings. Joe Brooks has always been fond of me. There!'

'Yeah,' he said. 'He's fond of you. He was so fond of you he didn't even send a wedding present. That's how fond of you he was.'

'I happen to know for a fact,' she said, 'that he was away on business, and as soon as he comes back he's going to give me anything I want, for the apartment.'

'Listen,' he said. 'I don't want anything he gives you in our apartment. Anything he gives you, I'll throw right out the window. That's what I think of your friend Joe Brooks. And how do you know where he is and what he's going to do, anyway? Has he been writing to you?'

'I suppose my friends can correspond with me,' she said. 'I didn't hear there was any law against that.'

'Well, I suppose they can't!' he said. 'And what do you think of that? I'm not going to have my wife getting a lot of letters from cheap travelling salesmen!'

'Joe Brooks is not a cheap travelling salesman!' she said. 'He is not! He gets a wonderful salary.'

'Oh yeah?' he said. 'Where did you hear that?'

'He told me so himself,' she said.

'Oh, he told you so himself,' he said. 'I see. He told you so himself.'

'You've got a lot of right to talk about Joe Brooks,' she said. 'You and your friend Louise. All you ever talk about is Louise.'

'Oh, for heaven's sakes!' he said. 'What do I care about Louise? I just thought she was a friend of yours, that's all. That's why I ever even noticed her.'

'Well, you certainly took an awful lot of notice of her today,' she said. 'On our wedding day! You said yourself when you were standing there in the church you just kept thinking of her. Right up at the altar. Oh, right in the presence of God! And all you thought about was Louise.'

'Listen, honey,' he said, 'I never should have said that. How does anybody know what kind of crazy things come into their heads when they're standing there waiting to get married? I was just telling you that because it was so kind of crazy. I thought it would make you laugh.'

'I know,' she said. 'I've been all sort of mixed up today, too. I told you that. Everything so strange and everything. And me all the time thinking about all those people all over the world, and now us here all alone, and everything. I know you get all mixed up. Only I did think, when you kept talking about how beautiful Louise looked, you did it with malice and forethought.'

'I never did anything with malice and forethought!' he said. 'I just told you that about Louise because I thought it would make you laugh.'

'Well, it didn't,' she said.

'No, I know it didn't,' he said. 'It certainly did not. Ah, baby, and we ought to be laughing, too. Hell, honey lamb, this is our honeymoon. What's the matter?'

'I don't know,' she said. 'We used to squabble a lot when we were going together and then engaged and everything, but I thought everything would be so different as soon as you were married. And now I feel so sort of strange and everything. I feel so sort of alone.'

'Well, you see, sweetheart,' he said, 'we're not really married yet. I mean. I mean – well, things will be different afterwards. Oh, hell. I mean, we haven't been married very long.'

'No,' she said.

'Well, we haven't got much longer to wait now,' he said. 'I mean – well, we'll be in New York in about twenty minutes. Then we can have dinner, and sort of see what we feel like doing. Or I mean. Is there anything special you want to do tonight?'

'What?' she said.

'What I mean to say,' he said, 'would you like to go to a show or something?'

'Why, whatever you like,' she said. 'I sort of didn't think

people went to theatres and things on their – I mean, I've got a couple of letters I simply must write. Don't let me forget.'

'Oh,' he said. 'You're going to write letters tonight?'

'Well, you see,' she said. 'I've been perfectly terrible. What with all the excitement and everything. I never did thank poor old Mrs Sprague for her berry spoon, and I never did a thing about those book ends the McMasters sent. It's just too awful of me. I've got to write them this very night.'

'And when you've finished writing your letters,' he said, 'maybe I could get you a magazine or a bag of peanuts.'

'What?' she said.

'I mean,' he said, 'I wouldn't want you to be bored.'

'As if I could be bored with you!' she said. 'Silly! Aren't we married? Bored!'

'What I thought,' he said, 'I thought when we got in, we could go right up to the Biltmore and anyway leave our bags, and maybe have a little dinner in the room, kind of quiet, and then do whatever we wanted. I mean. I mean – well, let's go right up there from the station.'

'Oh, yes, let's,' she said. 'I'm so glad we're going to the Biltmore. I just love it. The twice I've stayed in New York we've always stayed there, Papa and Mamma and Ellie and I, and I was crazy about it. I always sleep so well there. I go right off to sleep the minute I put my head on the pillow.'

'Oh, you do?' he said.

'At least, I mean,' she said. 'Way up high it's so quiet.'

'We might go to some show or other tomorrow night instead of tonight,' he said. 'Don't you think that would be better?'

'Yes, I think it might,' she said.

He rose, balanced a moment, crossed over and sat down beside her.

'Do you really have to write those letters tonight?' he said.

'Well,' she said, 'I don't suppose they'd get there any quicker than if I wrote them tomorrow.'

There was a silence with things going on in it.

'And we won't ever fight any more, will we?' he said.

'Oh, no,' she said. 'Not ever! I don't know what made me do like that. It all got so sort of funny, sort of like a nightmare, the way I got thinking of all those people getting married all the time; and so many of them, everything spoils on account of fighting and everything. I got all mixed up thinking about them. Oh, I don't want to be like them. But we won't be, will we?'

'Sure we won't,' he said.

'We won't go all to pieces,' she said. 'We won't fight. It'll all be different, now we're married. It'll all be lovely. Reach me down my hat, will you, sweetheart? It's time I was putting it on. Thanks. Ah, I'm so sorry you don't like it.'

'I do so like it!' he said.

'You said you didn't,' she said. 'You said you thought it was perfectly terrible.'

'I never said any such thing,' he said. 'You're crazy.'

'All right, I may be crazy,' she said. 'Thank you very much. But that's what you said. Not that it matters – it's just a little thing. But it makes you feel pretty funny to think you've gone and married somebody that says you have perfectly terrible taste in hats. And then goes and says you're crazy, beside.'

'Now, listen here,' he said. 'Nobody said any such thing. Why, I love that hat. The more I look at it the better I like it. I think it's great.'

'That isn't what you said before,' she said.

'Honey,' he said. 'Stop it, will you? What do you want to start all this for? I love the damned hat. I mean, I love your hat. I love anything you wear. What more do you want me to say?'

'Well, I don't want you to say it like that,' she said.

'I said I think it's great,' he said. 'That's all I said.'

'Do you really?' she said. 'Do you honestly? Ah, I'm so glad. I'd hate you not to like my hat. It would be – I don't know, it would be sort of such a bad start.'

'Well, I'm crazy for it,' he said. 'Now we've got that settled, for heaven's sakes. Ah, baby. Baby lamb. We're not going to have any bad starts. Look at us – we're on our honeymoon. Pretty soon we'll be regular old married people. I mean, in a few minutes we'll be getting in to New York, and then we'll be going to the hotel, and then everything will be all right. I mean – well, look at us! Here we are married! Here we are!'

'Yes, here we are,' she said. 'Aren't we?'

Two Hanged Women

Henry Handel Richardson

Hand in hand the youthful lovers sauntered along the esplanade. It was a night in midsummer; a wispy moon had set, and the stars glittered. The dark mass of the sea, at flood, lay tranquil, slothfully lapping the shingle.

'Come on, let's make for the usual,' said the boy.

But on nearing their favourite seat they found it occupied. In the velvety shade of the overhanging sea-wall, the outlines of two figures were visible.

'Oh, blast!' said the lad. 'That's torn it, What now, Baby?'

'Why, let's stop here, Pincher, right close up, till we frighten 'em off.'

And very soon loud, smacking kisses, amatory pinches and ticklings, and skittish squeals of pleasure did their work. Silently the intruders rose and moved away.

But the boy stood gaping after them, open-mouthed.

'Well, I'm *damned*! If it wasn't just two hanged women!'

Retreating before a salvo of derisive laughter, the elder of the girls said: 'We'll go out on the breakwater.' She was tall and thin, and walked with a long stride.

Her companion, shorter than she by a bobbed head of straight flaxen hair, was hard put to it to keep pace. As she pegged along she said doubtfully, as if in self-excuse: 'Though I really ought to go home. It's getting late. Mother will be angry.'

They walked with finger-tips lightly in contact; and at her words she felt what was like an attempt to get free, on the part of the fingers crooked in hers. But she was prepared for this, and held fast, gradually working her own up till she had a good half of the other hand in her grip.

For a moment neither spoke. Then, in a low muffled voice, came the question: 'Was she angry last night, too?'

The little fair girl's reply had an unlooked-for vehemence. 'You know she wasn't!' and mildly despairing: 'But you never *will* understand. Oh, what's the good of . . . of anything!'

And on sitting down she let the prisoned hand go, even putting it from her with a kind of push. There it lay, palm upwards, the fingers still curved from her hold, looking like a thing with a separate life of its own; but a life that was ebbing.

On this remote seat, with their backs turned on lovers, lights, the town, the two girls sat and gazed wordlessly at the dark sea, over which great Jupiter was flinging a thin gold line. There was no sound but the lapping, sucking, sighing, of the ripples at the edge of the breakwater, and the occasional screech of an owl in the tall trees on the hillside.

But after a time, having stolen more than one side-glance at her companion, the younger seemed to take heart of grace. With a childish toss of the head that set her loose hair swaying, she said, in a tone of meaning emphasis: 'I like Fred.'

The only answer was a faint, contemptuous shrug.

'I tell you, I *like* him!'

'Fred? Rats!'

'No it isn't . . . that's just where you're wrong, Betty. But you think you're so wise. Always.'

'I know what I know.'

'Or imagine you do! But it doesn't matter. Nothing you can say makes any difference. I like him, and always shall. In heaps of ways. He's so big and strong, for one thing: it gives you such a safe sort of feeling to be with him . . . as if nothing could happen while you were. Yes, it's . . . it's . . . well, I can't help it, Betty there's something *comfy* in having a boy to go about with – like other girls do. One they'd eat their hats to get, too! I can see it in their eyes when we pass; Fred with his great long legs and broad shoulders – I don't nearly come up to them – and his blue eyes with the black lashes, and his shiny black hair. And I like his tweeds, the Harris smell of them, and his dirty old pipe, and the way he shows his teeth – he's got *topping* teeth – when he laughs and says "ra-*ther*!" And other people, when they see us, look . . . well I don't know how to say it, but they look sort of pleased; and they make room for us and let us into the dark corner-seats at the pictures, just as if we'd a right to them. And they never laugh. (Oh, I can't *stick* being laughed at! – and that's the truth.) Yes, it's so comfy, Betty darling . . . such a warm cosy comfy feeling. Oh, *won't* you understand?'

'Gawd! why not make a song of it?' But a moment later, very fiercely: 'And who is it's taught you to think all this? Who's hinted it and suggested it till you've come to believe it? . . . believe it's what you really feel.'

'She hasn't! Mother's never said a word . . . about Fred.'

'Words? – why waste words? . . . when she can do it with a cock of the eye. For your Fred, that!' and the girl called Betty held her fingers aloft and snapped them viciously. 'But your mother's a different proposition.'

'I think you're simply horrid.'

To this there was no reply.

'*Why* have you such a down on her? What's she ever done to you? . . . except not get ratty when I stay out late with Fred. And I don't see how you can expect . . . being what she is . . . and with nobody but me . . . after all she *is* my mother . . . you can't alter that. I know very well – and you know, too – I'm not *too* putrid-looking. But' – beseechingly – 'I'm *nearly* twenty-five now, Betty. And other girls . . . well, she sees them every one of them, with a boy of their own, even though they're ugly or fat, or have legs like sausages – they've only got to ogle them a bit – the girls, I mean . . . and there they are. And Fred's a good sort – he is, really! – and he dances well, and doesn't drink, and so . . . so why *shouldn't* I like him? . . . and off my own bat . . . without it having to be all Mother's fault, and me nothing but a parrot, and without any will of my own?'

'Why? Because I know her too well, my child! I can read her as you'd never dare to . . . even if you could. She's sly, your mother is, so sly there's no coming to grips with her . . . one might as well try to fill one's hand with cobwebs. But she's got a hold on you, a stranglehold, that nothing'll loosen. Oh! mothers aren't fair – I mean it's not fair of nature to weigh us down with them and yet expect us to be our own true selves. The handicap's too great. All those months, when the same blood's running through two sets of veins – there's no getting away from that, ever after. Take yours. As I say, does she need to open her mouth? Not she! She's only got to let it hang at the corners, and you reek, you drip with guilt.'

Something in these words seemed to sting the younger girl. She hit back, 'I know what it is, you're jealous, that's what you are! . . . and you've no other way of letting it out. But I tell you this. If ever I marry – yes *marry*! – it'll be to please myself, and nobody else. Can you imagine me doing it to oblige her?'

Again silence.

'If I only think what it would be like to be fixed up and settled, and able to live in peace, without this eternal dragging two ways . . . just as if I was being torn in half. And see Mother smiling and happy again, like she used to be. Between the two of you I'm nothing but a punch-ball. Oh, I'm fed up with it! . . . fed up to the neck. As for you . . . And yet you can sit there as if you were made of stone! Why don't you *say* something? *Betty*! Why won't you speak?'

But no words came.

'I can *feel* you sneering. And when you sneer I hate you more than any one on earth. If only I'd never seen you!'

'Marry your Fred, and you'll never need to again.'

'I will, too! I'll marry him, and have a proper wedding like other girls, with a veil and bridesmaids and bushels of flowers. And I'll live in a house of my own, where I can do as I like, and be left in peace, and there'll be no one to badger and bully me – Fred wouldn't – ever! Besides, he'll be away all day. And when he came back at night, he'd . . . I'd . . . I mean I'd –' But here the flying words gave out; there came a stormy breath and a cry of: 'Oh, Betty, Betty! . . . I couldn't, no, I couldn't! It's when I think of *that* . . . Yes, it's quite true! I like him all right, I do indeed, but only as long as he doesn't come too near. If he even sits too close, I have to screw myself up to bear it' – and flinging herself down over her companion's lap, she hid her face. 'And if he tries to touch me, Betty, or even takes my arm or puts his around me . . . And then his face . . . when it looks like it does sometimes . . . all wrong . . . as if it had gone all wrong – oh! then I feel I shall have to scream – out loud. I'm afraid of him . . . when he looks like that. Once . . . when he kissed me . . . I could have died with the horror of it. His breath . . . his breath . . . and his mouth – like fruit pulp – and the black hairs on his wrists . . . and the way he looked – and . . . and everything! No, I can't, I can't . . . nothing will make me . . . I'd rather die twice over. But what am I to do? Mother'll *never* understand. Oh, why has it got to be like this? I want to be happy, too . . . and everything's all wrong. You tell me, Betty darling, you help me, you're older . . . you *know* . . . and you can help me, if you will . . . if you only will!' And locking her arms round her friend she drove her face deeper into the warmth and darkness, as if, from the very fervour of her clasp, she could draw the aid and strength she needed.

Betty had sat silent, unyielding, her sole movement being to loosen her own arms from her sides and point her elbows outwards, to hinder them touching the arms that lay round her. But at this last appeal, she melted; and gathering the young girl to her breast, she held her fast. – And so for long she continued to sit, her chin resting lightly on the fair hair, that was silky and downy as an infant's, and gazing with sombre eyes over the stealthily heaving sea.

The Lottery

Marjorie Barnard

The first that Ted Bilborough knew of his wife's good fortune was when one of his friends, an elderly wag, shook his hand with mock gravity and murmured a few words of manly but inappropriate sympathy. Ted didn't know what to make of it. He had just stepped from the stairway on to the upper deck of the 6.15 p.m. ferry from town. Fred Lewis seemed to have been waiting for him, and as he looked about he got the impression of newspapers and grins and a little flutter of half derisive excitement, all focused on himself. Everything seemed to bulge towards him. It must be some sort of leg-pull. He felt his assurance threatened, and the corner of his mouth twitched uncomfortably in his fat cheek, as he tried to assume a hard-boiled manner.

'Keep the change, laddie,' he said.

'He doesn't know, actually he doesn't know.'

'Your wife's won the lottery!'

'He won't believe you. Show him the paper. There it is as plain as my nose. Mrs Grace Bilborough, 52 Cuthbert Street.' A thick, stained forefinger pointed to the words. 'First prize £5000 Last Hope Syndicate.'

'He's taking it very hard,' said Fred Lewis, shaking his head.

They began thumping him on the back. He had travelled on that ferry every week-day for the last ten years, barring a fortnight's holiday in January, and he knew nearly everyone. Even those he didn't know entered into the spirit of it. Ted filled his pipe nonchalantly but with unsteady fingers. He was keeping that odd unsteadiness, that seemed to begin somewhere deep in his chest, to himself. It was a wonder that fellows in the office hadn't got hold of this, but they had been busy today in the hot loft under the chromium pipes of the pneumatic system, sending down change and checking up on credit accounts. Sale time. Grace might have let him know. She could have rung up from Thompson's. Bill was always borrowing the lawn mower and the step ladder, so it would hardly be asking a favour in the circumstances. But that was Grace all over.

'If I can't have it myself, you're the man I like to see get it.'

They meant it too. Everyone liked Ted in a kind sort of way. He was a good fellow in both senses of the word. Not namby pamby, always ready for a joke but a good citizen too, a good husband and father. He wasn't the sort that refused to wheel the perambulator. He flourished the perambulator. His wife could hold up her head, they paid their bills weekly and he even put something away, not much but something, and that was a triumph the way things were, the ten per cent knocked off his salary in the depression not restored yet, and one thing and another. And always cheerful, with a joke for everyone. All this was vaguely present in Ted's mind. He'd always expected in a trusting sort of way to be rewarded, but not through Grace.

'What are you going to do with it, Ted?'

'You won't see him for a week, he's going on a jag.' This was very funny because Ted never did, not even on Anzac Day.

A voice with a grievance said, not for the first time, 'I've had shares in a ticket every week since it started, and I've never won a cent.' No one was interested.

'You'll be going off for a trip somewhere?'

'They'll make you president of the Tennis Club and you'll have to donate a silver cup.'

They were flattering him underneath the jokes.

'I expect Mrs Bilborough will want to put some of it away for the children's future,' he said. It was almost as if he were giving an interview to the press, and he was pleased with himself saying the right thing. He always referred to Grace in public as Mrs Bilborough. He had too nice a social sense to say 'the Missus'.

Ted let them talk, and looked out of the window. He wasn't interested in the news in the paper tonight. The little boat vibrated fussily, and left a long wake like moulded glass in the quiet river. The evening was drawing in. The sun was sinking into a bank of grey cloud, soft and formless as mist. The air was dusky, so that its light was closed into itself and it was easy to look at, a thick golden disc more like a moon rising through smoke than the sun. It threw a single column of orange light on the river, the ripples from the ferry fanned out into it, and their tiny shadows truncated it. The bank, rising steeply from the river and closing it in till it looked like a lake, was already bloomed with shadows. The shapes of two churches and a broken frieze of pine trees stood out against the gentle sky, not sharply, but with a soft arresting grace. The slopes, wooded and scattered with houses, were dim and sunk in idyllic peace. The river showed thinly bright against the dark land. Ted could see that the smooth water was really a pale tawny gold with patches, roughened by the turning tide, of frosty blue. It was only when you stared at it and concentrated your attention that you realized the colours. Turning to look downstream away from the sunset, the water gleamed silvery grey with dark clear scrabblings upon it. There were two worlds, one looking towards the sunset with the dark land against it dreaming and still, and the other looking downstream over the silvery river to the other bank, on which all the light concentrated. Houses with windows of orange fire, black trees, a great silver gasometer, white oil tanks with the look of clumsy mushrooms, buildings serrating the sky, even a suggestion seen or imagined of red roofs, showing up miraculously in that airy light.

'Five thousand pounds,' he thought. 'Five thousand pounds.' Five thousand pounds at five per cent, five thousand pounds stewing gently away in its interest, making old age safe. He could do almost anything he could think of with five thousand pounds. It gave his mind a stretched sort of feeling, just thinking of it. It was hard to connect five thousand pounds with Grace. She might have let him know. And where had the five and threepence to buy the ticket come from? He couldn't help wondering about that. When you budgeted as carefully as they did there wasn't five and threepence over. If there had been, well, it wouldn't have been over at all, he would have put it in the bank. He hadn't noticed any difference in the housekeeping, and he prided himself he noticed everything. Surely she hadn't been running up bills to buy lottery tickets. His mind darted here and there suspiciously. There was something secretive in Grace, and he'd thought she told him everything. He'd taken it for granted, only, of course, in the ordinary run there was nothing to tell. He consciously relaxed the knot in his mind. After all, Grace had won the five thousand pounds. He remembered charitably that she had always been a good wife to him. As he thought that he had a vision of the patch on his shirt, his newly-washed cream trousers laid for tennis, the children's neatness, the tidy house. That was being a good wife. And he had been a good husband, always brought his money home and never looked at another woman. Theirs was a model home, everyone acknowledged it, but – well – somehow he found it easier to be cheerful in other people's homes than in his own. It was Grace's fault. She wasn't cheery and easy going. Something moody about her now. Woody. He'd worn better than Grace, anyone could see that, and yet it was he who had had the hard time. All she had to do was to stay at home and look after the house and the children. Nothing much in that. She always seemed to be working, but he couldn't see what there was to do that could take her so long. Just a touch of woman's perversity. It wasn't that Grace had aged. Ten years married and with two children, there was still something girlish about her – raw, hard girlishness that had never mellowed. Grace was – Grace, for better or for worse. Maybe she'd be a bit brighter now. He could not help wondering how she had managed the five and three. If she could shower five and threes about like that, he'd been giving her too much of the housekeeping. And why did she want to give it that damnfool name 'Last Hope.' That meant there had been others, didn't it? It probably didn't mean a thing, just a lucky tag.

A girl on the seat opposite was sewing lace on silkies for her trousseau, working intently in the bad light.

'Another one starting out,' Ted thought.

'What about it?' said the man beside him.

Ted hadn't been listening.

The ferry had tied up at his landing stage and Ted got off. He tried not to show in his walk that his wife had won £5000. He felt jaunty and tired at once. He walked up the hill with a bunch of other men, his neighbours. They were still teasing him about the money, they didn't know how to stop. It was a very still, warm evening. As the sun descended into the misty bank on the horizon it picked out the delicate shapes of clouds invisibly sunk in the mass, outlining them with a fine thread of gold.

One by one the men dropped out, turning into side streets or opening garden gates till Ted was alone with a single companion, a man who lived in a semi-detached cottage at the end of the street. They were suddenly very quiet and sober. Ted felt the ache round his mouth where he'd been smiling and smiling.

'I'm awfully glad you've had this bit of luck.'

'I'm sure you are, Eric,' Ted answered in a subdued voice.

'There's nobody I'd sooner see have it.'

'That's very decent of you.'

'I mean it.'

'Well, well, I wasn't looking for it.'

'We could do with a bit of luck like that in our house.'

'I bet you could.'

'There's an instalment on the house due next month, and Nellie's got to come home again. Seems as if we'd hardly done paying for the wedding.'

'That's bad.'

'She's expecting, so I suppose Mum and Dad will be let in for all that too.'

'It seems only the other day Nellie was a kid getting round on a scooter.'

'They grow up,' Eric agreed. 'It's the instalment that's the rub. First of next month. They expect it on the nail too. If we hadn't that hanging over us it wouldn't matter about Nellie coming home. She's our girl, and it'll be nice to have her about the place again.'

'You'll be as proud as a cow with two tails when you're a grandpa.'

'I suppose so.'

They stood mutely by Eric's gate. An idea began to flicker in Ted's mind, and with it a feeling of sweetness and happiness and power such as he had never expected to feel.

'I won't see you stuck, old man,' he said.

'That's awfully decent of you.'

'I mean it.'

They shook hands as they parted. Ted had only a few steps more and he took them slowly. Very warm and dry, he thought. The garden will need watering. Now he was at his gate. There was no one in sight. He stood for a moment looking about him. It was as if he saw the house he had lived in for ten years, for the first time. He saw that it had a mean, narrow-chested appearance. The roof tiles were discoloured, the woodwork needed painting, the crazy pavement that he had laid with such zeal had an unpleasant flirtatious look. The revolutionary thought formed in his mind. 'We might leave here.' Measured against the possibilities that lay before him, it looked small and mean. Even the name, 'Emoh Ruo,' seemed wrong, pokey.

Ted was reluctant to go in. It was so long since anything of the least importance had happened between him and Grace, that it made him shy. He did not know how she would take it? Would she be all in a dither and no dinner ready? He hoped so but feared not.

He went into the hall, hung up his hat and shouted in a big bluff voice, 'Well, well, well, and where's my rich wife?'

Grace was in the kitchen dishing dinner.

'You're late,' she said. 'The dinner's spoiling.'

The children were quiet but restless, anxious to leave the table and go out to play. 'I got rid of the reporters,' Grace said in a flat voice. Grace had character, trust her to handle a couple of cub reporters. She didn't seem to want to talk about it to her husband either. He felt himself, his voice, his stature dwindling. He looked at her with hard eyes. 'Where did she get the money?' he wondered again, but more sharply.

Presently they were alone. There was a pause. Grace began to clear the table. Ted felt that he must do something. He took her awkwardly into his arms. 'Grace, aren't you pleased?'

She stared at him a second then her face seemed to fall together, a sort of spasm, something worse than tears. But she twitched away from him. 'Yes,' she said, picking up a pile of crockery and making for the kitchen. He followed her.

'You're a dark horse, never telling me a word about it.'

'She's like a Red Indian,' he thought. She moved about the kitchen with quick nervous movements. After a moment she answered what was in his mind:

'I sold my mother's ring and chain. A man came to the door buying old gold. I bought a ticket every week till the money was gone.'

'Oh,' he said. Grace had sold her mother's wedding ring to buy a lottery ticket.

'It was my money.'

'I didn't say it wasn't.'

'No, you didn't.'

The plates clattered in her hands. She was evidently feeling something, and feeling it strongly. But Ted didn't know what. He couldn't make her out.

She came and stood in front of him, her back to the littered table, her whole body taut. 'I suppose you're wondering what I am going to do? I'll tell you. I'm going away. By myself. Before it's too late. I'm going tomorrow.'

He didn't seem to be taking it in.

'Beattie will come and look after you and the children. She'll be glad to. It won't cost you a penny more than it does now,' she added.

He stood staring at her, his flaccid hands hanging down, his face sagging.

'Then you meant what you said in the paper. "Last Hope?"' he said.

'Yes,' she answered.

Daughter

Anne McCaffrey

The moment her father began to yell at her twin brother Nick, Nora Fenn edged toward the door of the Complex office. George Fenn's anger always seemed to expand in direct proportion to the number of witnesses. She knew it humiliated Nick to be harangued in front of anyone, and this time there was absolutely nothing she could say in Nick's defence. Why hadn't he waited till she got back from school and could help him programme the Planter?

'Fifty acres clearly marked corn,' and Father viciously stabbed a thick forefinger at the corner of the room dominated by the scale model of the farm. He'd spent hours last winter rearranging the movable field units. In fact, Nora thought he displayed a lot more concern for the proper allocation of crops than he did for his two children. He certainly didn't berate the corn when the ears weren't plump or turned to ergot.

'And you,' roared Father, suddenly clamping his hands tightly to his sides, as if he were afraid of the damage they'd do if he didn't, '*you* plant turnips. What kind of programmer are you, Nicholas? A simple chore even your sister could do!'

Nora flinched at that. If Father ever found out that it was she, not Nick, who did the most complex programming . . . She eased past the county maps, careful not to rustle the thin sheets of plastic overlay that Father had marked with crop, irrigation, and fertilizing patterns. The office was not small. One wall, of course, was the computer console and storage banks, then the window that looked out on to the big yard of the Complex, the three-foot-square relief model of the Fenn Farmlands on its stand. But two angry Fenns would diminish a Bargaining Hall.

Nora was struck by a resemblance between father and son, which she'd not really appreciated before. Not only were both men holding their arms stiffly against their sides, but their jaws were set at the same obstinate angle and each held one shoulder slightly higher than the other.

'I'm going to see that so-called Guidance Counsellor of yours tomorrow and find out what kind of abortive computer courses you've been given. I thought I'd made it plain what electives you were to take.'

'I get the course I'm able to absorb . . .'

Oh, please, Nick, breathed Nora, don't argue with him. The Educational Advancements will be posted in a day, two at the most, and then there's nothing he can do to alter the decision.

'Fenns are landsmen,' Father shouted. 'Born to the land, bred by the land!'

The dictum reverberated through the room, and Nora used the noise to mask the slipping sound of the office door. She was out in the narrow passageway before Father realized that he'd lost part of his audience. She half ran to the outer door, the spongy-fibre floor masking the sounds of her booted feet. When she was safely outside the rambling trilevel habitation, she breathed with relief. She'd better finish her own after-school chores. Now that Father'd got started on Nick, he'd be finding fault elsewhere. Since there weren't any apprentice landsmen on the Fenn Farm Complex right now, 'elsewhere' could only be Nora. Mother never came in for Father's criticism, because everything she did in her quiet unspectacular way was perfectly done. Nora sighed. It wasn't fair to be so good at everything. When her children complained Mary Fenn would laugh and remark that practice made perfect. But Mother always had some bit of praise, or a hug or a kiss to hearten you when she knew you'd *tried*. Father . . . if Father would only say something encouraging to Nick . . .

Nora stayed to the left of the low, rambling, living quarters, out of the view afforded by the office window. She glanced across the huge plasti-cobbled yard which she had just finished hosing down. Yes, she had washed down the bay doors of the enormous barn that housed the Complex's Seeder, Plowboy and Harvester. And done a thorough job of cleaning the tracks on which the heavy equipment was shunted out of the yard and on to the various rails leading to the arable tracts.

Turnips! If only Nick had blown the job with a high-priority vegetable, like carrots or beets. But turnips? They were nothing but subsistence-level food. Father cannily complied with Farm Directives and still managed to plant most of the Fenn lands to creditable crops like corn and beets. Fifty more acres of turnips this year might mean Nick would have that much less free credit at the university.

Nora sighed. When Educational Advancements were posted, the suspense would be over, the pressure off the graduating students. Who'd go on to Applied or Academic in her class, she wondered? But there was no way of finding out short of stealing Fremmeng's wrist recorder. You only got pass/fail decisions in elementary grades. An arbitrary percentile evaluation defeated the purpose of modern educational methods. Achievement must be measured by individual endeavour, not mean averages or sliding curves. Young citizens were taught to know that knowledge was required of contributing citizens. Computer-assisted drill constantly checked on comprehension of concept and use of basic skills. Educational Advancement, either Applied or Academic, depended as much on demonstrated diligence as inherent ability. Consequently, the slow student had every bit as much chance, and just as much right to education as the quick learner.

Well, Nora told herself briskly, it doesn't contribute anything to society to stand here daydreaming. You'll know in a day or two. In the meantime . . .

Nora went through the grape arbour toward the skimmer shed, near the far left compound wall. She had just turned in to the building when she felt the reverberation of rapid thudding through the linked plasti-cobbles. Then Nick came pounding around the side of the building.

'Nora, lend me your skimmer?' he begged, unracking it as he spoke. 'Mine's still drying out from Saturday's irrigating.'

'But, Nick . . . Father . . .'

Nick's face darkened the way Father's did when he met resistance.

'Don't give me any static, Nor. I gotta change state . . .'

'Oh, Nick, *why* didn't you wait until I could've checked you out?'

Nick set his jaw, his eyes blinking rapidly.

'You had to see Fremmeng, remember? And when I got home, the orders were waiting and I couldn't. I'm due over at Felicity's *now*.' Nick turned up the pressure gauge, filling the tanks of the skimmer. 'Orders. Orders. That's all I ever get from him. That and "Fenns are crop farmers."' Nick snorted. 'He thinks he can programme kids like a computer. Well, I'm *not* a crop farmer. It switches me off. Off!'

'Nick, please. Keep unity. Once you get to the university, *you* choose the courses you want. He can't go against Educational Advancement. And if he tries, you can always claim sanctuary against parental coercion. There isn't anyone in the Sector who wouldn't support your claim . . .'

Nick was staring at her incredulously, but suddenly the anger drained out of his face and was replaced by an exaggerated expression of tolerant forbearance.

'Claim sanctuary? I haven't lost all sense of unity, Nora,' he told her sternly. 'Hey, what did Fremmeng want *you* for?'

'Me? Oh, he had the most absolutely irrelevant questions! About how you and I get along, my opinions on family harmony and social contributions, and pairing off.'

Nick regarded her with an intent, impersonal stare.

'He did, huh? Look, Nor,' and her brother's mood changed state completely, 'I need to see Felicity. I gotta blow out of *here*!'

Nora grabbed his arm as he inflated the skimmer.

'Nick, what *did* you say to Father?'

Nick gave her a sour look now. 'I told him he'd better hold off making so many big plans for me to be the Fenn Complex's Master Ruralist, until he sees the Educational Advancements.'

'Nick, if you don't get Advancement, Father will just . . . just . . .'

'Abort and sulk!' Nick finished for her. 'No, I'll get Advancement, all right. On my terms! There's not a blasted thing wrong with Applied. It's Father who tried programming the university for me. But I've had different plans.' Nick's look turned as hard as flint.

'What do you mean, Nick? What have you been doing?'

Nora was suddenly scared. What had Father driven Nick to do?

'Nora, sweetie, Old Bates at the Everett Complex is about due for retirement. Felicity Everett and I want to pair off as soon as the EAs have been posted. And it's just possible that Landsman Everett would opt for me as assistant.' Nick's expression altered again, this time to enthusiasm, and Nora felt relief at the change.

'Oh, he would, Nick. You know what he said about your term paper on ovine gene manipulation.' Then Nora caught the significance of his plan.

'Yes, indeedy, sister mine. Nick can cut a programme on his own, without your help or Father's.'

She was so astonished at the calculation in his smile that he was able to loosen her fingers from the handlebars. He was off on the skimmer at a high blow before she could stop him.

'Nick . . .'

'Give my love to our foul-feathered friends!' he called over his shoulder cheerfully, and launched the skimmer straight across the meadows toward the Everetts' Herd Complex.

Resolutely, Nora made for the distant Poultry House on foot. Father proclaimed that chickens and turkeys were a woman's business. She hated tending them and usually swapped the chore with Nick. Nick found poultry a trifle more engrossing than the tedious crop programming.

Why couldn't Nick focus a little more attention on what he was doing instead of expending all his energies thwarting Father? Irritably, she scuffed at a vagrant pebble in the track that led straight from the low-rambling Farm Complex, set in the fold of the soft hills, toward the Poultry House. She could see the glitter of the round roof as she topped the next rise.

Educational Advancement! She so hoped that she'd qualify . . . at least for Applied Advancement. That would prove to Father she wasn't all that stupid, even if she was a girl. Maybe, if she could make Journeyman Class Computer . . . she really felt that she understood mathematics and symbolic logic. If she got Journeyman, Father mightn't be so disappointed when he finally realized that Nick was absolutely set against crop farming. While Father might feel that women were being educated far beyond society's profit, no contributing citizen could argue with the Advancement Board's decision. For the board was impartial, having the best interests of society *and* the individual at heart. Father might scoff at the premise that everyone had the constitutional right to shelter, food, clothing, *and* education as long as he maintained a class average. But then, Father disparaged a system that rewarded the diligent student with credit bonuses for something as intangible as academic excellence.

'That doesn't feed anyone, make anything, buy or sell anything,' he'd say when he'd started on that tangent. There was no use explaining to such a pragmatist.

If Nora could get certified in computer logistics and was able to handle the Complex's Master Ruralist; then surely he'd be proud of her. He wouldn't mind that one of his children was a girl, not the second boy *he'd* printed into the Propagation Registration.

Father never let Nora, or her mother, forget that he had not computed twins, nor mixed sexes. *He'd* opted for both legal progeny to be male. Since early sex education in school, Nora had wondered how her mother had managed not only a multiple birth but a split in sexes without Father's knowledge. For one thing, multiple births had been uncommon for the last hundred years, since Population Control had been initiated. Most duly registered couples opted for one of each sex, well spaced. Of course, George Fenn would complain about PC, too. Or rather, the provision which permitted only exceptional couples to have one or two more children above the legal number – in return for extraordinary contributions to society.

'They put the emphasis on the wrong genetic factors,' Father would argue bitterly whenever the subject came up. 'If you breed for brain, the species weakens physically, flaws develop.' He'd always flex his huge biceps then, show off his two-metre-tall, one-hundred-kilo frame in support of his argument. He'd been disappointed, too, when Nick, scarcely an undersized man, stopped slightly short of two metres in height. Father'd glower at Nora, as if her slender body had robbed her twin of extra centimetres.

How had Mary Fenn, a woman of muted qualities, coped so long and amiably with her husband? Her quiet, uncritical voice was seldom raised. She knew when you were upset, though, or sick, and her capable hands were sure and soft. If anyone deserved Maternity Surplus, it was Mother. She was so good! And she'd managed to remain completely in control of herself, a presence unperturbed by her husband's tirades and intemperate attitudes, efficiently dealing with each season and its exigencies.

Of course, it was no wonder that Mother was quiet. Father was such a dominating person. He could shout down an entire Rural Sector Meeting.

'A fine landsman,' Nora heard her father called. 'But don't cross him,' she'd heard whispered. 'He'll try to programme things his way, come hell or high water. He knows the land, though,' was the grudging summation.

'Knows the land, but not humans,' Nora muttered under her breath. 'Not his children. Certainly he doesn't know what his son really wants.'

Maybe once Nick gets away to university, harmony will be restored between father and son. Nick ought to have a stronger desire to maintain family unity . . .

Crop farming wasn't all that bad, Nora thought. By punching the right buttons, you could now mow a thousand-acre field, as Nora had done as a pre-teen, when the apprentices let her. You could winnow and cull with a vacuum attachment; grade, bag, clean your field far more efficiently than the most careful ancient gleaners. You could programme your Plowboy to fertilize at five levels as the seed was replanted. One Complex with two families or a couple of responsible apprentices could efficiently farm an old-time country-sized spread and still turn a luxury credit. Not to mention having fresh and ready supplies of any edible and some of those luxuries above the subsistence level that the City Complexes craved.

Now Nora could hear the pitiful muted honking of the geese in the Poultry House. She winced. There were certain aspects of farming that could not be completely automated. You can't tape a broody hen, and you can't computerize the services of a rooster. Cocks' crows still heralded sunrise over the fields, whether the clarion summons issued from a wooden slated crate or the sleek multipentangle that housed the poultry raised by the Fenn Complex. Eggs laid by hens in Nora's charge would be powdered and eventually whipped to edibility on the Jupiter station, or be flash-frozen to provide sustenance when the first colony ship set forth as it was rumoured to do in the next decade. Turkeys from this Complex regularly made the one-way trip to the Moon bases for Winter Solstice celebrations, call them Saturnalias or Santa Claus if you would.

She entered the poultry pentangle through the access tunnel which led straight to the computer core that handled all watering, feeding, cleaning, egg collection, and slaughter operations. The Fenn Complex did not sell to dietary groups, so the market preparations were the standard ones.

She checked the tapes on the Leghorn fifth, replenished the grit supply, and tapped out a re-order sequence. She flushed out all the pen floors and refreshed the water. Then she checked the mean weight of the tom turkeys, growing from scrawny, long-legged adolescence to plump-breasted maturity. A trifle more sand for digestion, a richer mash for firmer meats, and a little less of the growth hormones. Concentrated goodness, not size for size's sake any more.

The geese were fattening, too, on their fixed perches. Goose livers on the rod. Nora hated the calculated cruelty that brought in credit margin for the Fenn Complex. Stuff the poor helpless fowl, engorge their livers for the delectation of the gourmet. The geese lived sheltered, circumscribed lives, which was not living at all, for they couldn't see out of their own quarters. Nothing distracted them from their purpose in life – death from enlarged livers. Nora was distracted from her chores by their shrill honking. She forced herself to read the gauges. Yes, the upper group were ready for market. Even their plaint registered the truth of their self-destruction. They'd been bred for one purpose. It was their time to fulfil it. She coldly dialled for a quotation on the price of geese and goose liver at the Central Farm Exchange. The European price printed out at a respectable high. She routed the information to the Farm's main console. It might just sweeten Father's cantankerous mood to realize a quick credit from the sale.

Nora took a detour on the way back, across the one-hundred-acre field. The willows her great-grandfather had planted the day the Farm Reforms were passed were tipped with raw yellow. Spring was an Earth-moment away. Soon the golden limbs would sprout their green filaments, to drape and float them on the irrigation ditch that watered their thirsty feet. Would *her* great-grandchildren admire the willows in their turn? The whimsy irritated her.

She walked faster, away from what the willows stood for. She didn't really have to be back at the Complex until mealtime, an hour or so away. Father always programmed too much time for her to tend the poultry house, which was an unflattering assessment of her ability but usually gave her more time for something she'd wanted to do that Father might not consider contributory. If only *once* he'd look at her as if she weren't something printed out by mistake. How in the name of little printed circuits had Mother dared to have twins?

Nora used her spare time to pick cress at the sluice gate beds. It was a soothing occupation and contributed to dinner's salad. When she finally got back to the house, she glanced into the office. The printout slot was clear, so Father had seen her report. She'd simply have to wait to find out if he'd acted on the data. The main console was keyed to his code only.

She heard the meal chime from the kitchen area and quickly brought the cress to her mother, who was taking roast lamb out of the oven. Did Mother know about Nick's quarrel? Lamb was her father's favourite protein.

'Oh, cress! That was a considerate thought, Nora. We'll put a few sprigs on the lamb platter for looks. There'll only be three of us for dinner, you know.'

Nora didn't know, for surely Nick would be back from the Everett Complex; but just then Father came in, grim-faced, and sat down. Again Nora wondered just how far he had goaded Nick this afternoon. Why had she played the coward and left?

The tender lamb stuck in her throat like so much dry feed. Her stomach seemed to close up as if eating had been programmed out, but she forced herself to clear her plate. No one, in this day and age and especially at George Fenn's table, wasted real food. Once – and only once – as a child she had left real food on her plate. She'd spent the next two weeks trying to swallow common subsistence-level rations.

Conversation was never encouraged at Fenn meals, so the

awkward meal dragged on. When Nora could finally excuse herself and make for the sanctuary of her room, her father stopped her.

'So, Nora, you've been doing Nicholas's programming for him, eh?' Father's voice was icy with disapproval; his eyes were specks of grey.

Nora stared back, speechless. Oh, Nick couldn't have!

'Don't gawk at me, girl. Answer!' Father's big fist banged the table and a startled 'Yes, Father,' came from her.

'And how long has this . . . this deception gone on?'

Nora didn't dare look at him.

'How long?' Father repeated, his voice rising in volume and getting sharper.

'Since – since spring,' she answered.

'*Which* spring?' was the acid query.

Nora swallowed hard against the sudden nauseating taste of lamb in her mouth.

'The first year of programming.'

'You *dared* take over a task assigned your brother – by me? Designed to acquaint him with the problems he'll face as a landsman?'

Instinctively Nora leaned as far back in her chair, away from her father's looming body, as she could. Not even George Fenn would disrupt family harmony by striking a child, but he was so angry that it seemed to Nora he had become a terrible stranger, capable even of causing her physical harm.

'Nick couldn't seem to get the trick of it,' she managed to say in her own defence. 'I only helped a little. When he got jammed.'

'He's a Fenn. He's got farming in his blood. Five generations of farming. You've robbed him of his heritage, of his proper contribu–'

'Oh, no, Father. Nick's always contributed. He'd do the poultry . . .' and her sentence broke off as she saw the bloated, red face of her father.

'You dared – *dared* exchange assignments?'

'You miss the point entirely, George,' Mother interceded in her placid way. 'The tasks were completed, were well done, so I cannot see why it is so wrong for Nick to have done which, and Nora what. They're both Fenns, after all. That's the core of the matter.'

'Have you changed state, woman?' Father wanted to know, but astonishment had aborted his anger. 'Nicholas is my son! Nora's only a girl.'

'Really, George. Don't quibble. You know, I've been thinking of enlarging my contribution to society now that the children are about to advance. I'd really like to go back to the Agriculture Institute and update my credentials. Sometimes,' Mother went on in the conversational way in which she was apt to deliver startling conclusions, 'I think the children have studied a whole new language when I hear them discussing computer logic. Remember when I used to take an apprentice's place, George? Of course, it would be much more interesting for me if you'd diversity the Complex. I can't have any more children, of course, but if we bred lambs or calves, I'd've young things to tend again. Society does say it'll satisfy every individual's needs.' She gave her husband an appealing smile. 'Do try to compute that in your fall programme, George. I'd appreciate it.'

Looking at Mother as if she'd taken leave of her senses, Father rose and pushed back his chair. He mumbled something about checking urgent data, but stumbled out of the dining area, past the office, and out of the house.

'Mother, I'd no idea . . .'

The rest of Nora's words died in her throat because her mother's eyes were brimming with mischief and she looked about to laugh.

'I oughtn't to do that to George when he's had a big dinner. But there're more ways to kill a cat than choking him with butter – as my grandmother used to say. Although that's a shocking way to use butter – not to mention a good cat – but Grandmother was full of such dairy-oriented expressions. Hmmmm. Now dairy farming might not be such a bad compromise, considering the printout quotes on milk and cheese this spring.' Then she closed her lips firmly as if her own loquacity startled her as much as it did Nora. The laughter died in her eyes. 'Nora?'

'Yes, Mother?'

'In this society, a person is legally permitted to develop at his own pace and follow his own aptitudes. Not even a stubborn atavist like your father has the right to inhibit another's contribution. Of course, the responsible citizen tries to maintain harmonious relations with his family unit up to that point of interference.

'You realized, I'm certain, that even if Nick has no love of crop farming, he is basically attuned to rural life. I've been so grateful to you, dear, for . . . soothing matters between your father and brother.' The words came out haltingly and though Mother didn't look directly at her, Nora could appreciate her difficulty. Mother had scrupulously avoided taking sides in the constant altercations between Nick and Father. She had somehow always maintained family unity. Her unexpected frankness was essentially a betrayal of that careful neutrality. 'I had hoped that Nick might be a more biddable boy, able to go along with his father's ambitions. They may be old-fashioned –'

'Mother, you *know* Father is positively medieval at times.' Nora regretted her flippancy when she saw the plea for understanding in her mother's eyes. 'Well, he is, but that's his bit. And he does make a distinguished contribution as a landsman.'

'Yes, Nora. Few men these days have your father's real love of the earth. It isn't every landsman,' Mother added, her voice proud, 'who runs a Complex as big as ours and makes a creditable balance.'

'If only Father didn't *try* . . .'

But Mother was looking off into the middle distance, her face so troubled, her eyes so dark with worry, that Nora wanted to cry out that she really did understand. Hadn't she proved that with all she'd done to keep unity?

'You're a kind, thoughtful, considerate child, Nora,' Mother said finally, smiling with unexpected tenderness. 'You undoubtedly rate very high on interpersonal relationships.'

'You must, too,' Nora protested, glancing toward the office.

Mother gave a rueful little laugh. 'I do, or I shouldn't have got on so well with your father all these years. But, right now, we both have to work together to maintain family harmony.'

'You haven't had a deficiency notice on me, have you?'

'Good lands, no child,' and Mother was clearly startled at

the notion. 'But Nick had an interview with Counsellor Fremmeng and he's reasonably certain, from the way the Counsellor talked, that he is going to disappoint your father. You know that George has been positive Nick would receive Academic Advancement. And frankly, Nora, Nick not only doesn't want it, he's sure he won't get it.'

'Yes, he mentioned something like that to me this afternoon after Father reamed him,' Nora said sadly. 'But what could Father possibly do in the face of EA postings except admit that he couldn't compute Nick into his own programme?'

Mother gave Nora one of her long, disconcertingly candid stares.

'It's not a question, Nora, of what your Father would or would not do. It's a question of how we maintain family unity, and your father's dignity and standing in the Sector. With a little tactful and affectionate . . . handling, he can think it was all his own notion in the first place.'

Nora stared at her mother with dawning respect and admiration.

'That's why you offered to update your credentials?'

Mother grinned. 'Just thought I'd plant the notion. It *is* spring, you know.'

'Mother, why on earth did you marry Father?' Nora asked in a rush. She might never get another chance to find out.

An unexpectedly tender expression on her mother's face made her appear younger, prettier.

'Land's sake, because he was the kind of man I wanted to marry,' Mary Fenn said with a proud lift of her chin. 'A man to do for, and George takes a lot of doing, you know. Keeps me on my toes. He has such tremendous vitality. I like that. He knows and loves and understands the land, and I wanted that, too. I knew that was good for me, to be close to the land, and I wanted to raise my children close to natural things. Sometimes I think there's too much dependence on technology. I'm a throwback, too, Nora, just as much as your father is with his antiquated notions of a son following in his father's footsteps on land that's been in the same family for generations.' Mother looked down at her square-palmed strong-fingered hands as if they represented her inner self. 'I like to feel warm earth, to get dirty. I want to *do* with my hands, not just let them idly punch a button or two. I like growing things, young things. If I could've defied the Population Control laws, too. I'd've had a whole passel of brats to raise. As it was . . .' and her lips formed a glowing smile of love and compassion that could encompass a whole country.

'As it was,' Nora giggled, 'you had twins in spite of Father.'

'Yes,' Mary Fenn chuckled, her eyes lit up with laughter, 'I had twins. A boy for your father,' and her face was both dutiful and mischievous, 'and a girl for me.'

'Well, Nick's not the son Father wanted. Mother –' and suddenly the answer was the most important thing in Nora's life. '– Mother, am I the daughter *you* wanted?'

The laughter died abruptly and Mother placed her square hands on either side of Nora's face.

'You're a good child, Nora. You never complain. You work hard and willingly. Yes, you're a good daughter.'

But that wasn't the answer Nora wanted.

'But what do *you* want me to *be*?'

'Happy, Nora. I want you to be happy.' Mary Fenn turned, then, to glance around the kitchen area, checking to see if all was in order. It was a dismissal, a tacit gesture not to pursue this subject further. Her mother often did that. Particularly with Father. She didn't actually evade a question, simply didn't answer it directly or fully.

'Mother, that isn't enough of an answer any more.'

Her mother turned back to her, her eyebrows raised in a polite question that turned to a frown when she'd studied her daughter's stern face.

'I only wanted a daughter, Nora, not a child in my own image, to follow in my path. Just a girl child to raise, to love, to delight in. A woman is proud to bear her son, but she rejoices in her daughter. You've given me much secret joy, Nora. I'm proud of you for many, silly little motherly reasons you'll understand when you have your own daughter. Beyond that . . .' Mother began to move away. 'I believe that everyone must be allowed to determine his own life's course. In that respect I am completely modern. Do *you* dislike farm life as much as your brother, Nora?'

'No,' but Nora realized as she said it that she was no longer sure. 'It's not that I dislike it, Mother, it's just that I'd prefer to do something more . . .'

'More cerebral, less manual?' her mother asked teasingly.

Nora could feel the blush mounting in her cheeks. She didn't want Mother to think she felt farming wasn't a substantial contribution.

'Well,' and her mother's voice was brisk again, 'the Advancements will soon be posted. They'll decide the matter once and for all. In the meantime –'

'I'll be a good daughter.'

'I know I can count on you,' and there was a sudden worried edge to her mother's voice. 'Now go. You've studying, I know. You want to achieve a good credit bonus at graduation.'

Nora let her mother's gentle shove propel her toward the ramp up to the bedroom level. But she was far too disquieted to study. Her mother had never been so forthright, and yet Nora did not feel the reassurance which ought to have resulted from such frankness.

There'd been many nuances in the conversation, emotional undertones which her mother had never permitted her daughter to hear before. And so many shifts. Almost as if Mother had really been sounding her out. On what? Useless to examine emotions: they were too subjective. They weren't computable data.

Nora tapped out a request for a mathematics review, senior level, on her home-study console. She was still staring at the first problem, when the computer pinged warningly and then chattered out the answer. Nora turned off the console and sat staring at the printout.

Was she really the daughter Mary Fenn had wanted? How would she ever know? She was certainly not the second son her father had intended to sire, though she had all the capabilities he'd wanted. If Nick wouldn't crop farm the Fenn Complex, how were they going to get Father to accept a compromise? Maybe Mother wanted her to prove to Father that she knew more about crop farming than Nick right now? No, George Fenn wanted his *son* to follow him at Fenn Complex. If not Nick, then some man, because George Fenn's atavistic temperament required him to pass land to a man, not a woman, even of his own genetic heritage.

This year's apprentices would be assigned here soon, fresh from their courses in Applied Agriculture at the Institute.

Maybe she'd like one of them, pair off with him, and then the Fenn land would at least remain in partially Fenn hands for another generation. Was this what Mother had been hinting at when she mentioned Nora's rating in IPR?

No, the trick would be to get Father to agree to diversify. That way Nick, who was just as stubborn as his father, could follow his heart's desire and society would benefit all around. But, when Mother brought that notion up at mealtime, Father had rushed out of the house as if his circuits had jammed.

Nora looked disconsolately down at the console. Within the parameters of the programming, computers reacted to taped instructions, facts that could be ineradicably stored as minute bits in their memories. Only humans put no parameters on dreams and stored aspirations.

The sound of a vehicle braking to a stop broke into her thoughts. Nick had come back!

The angle of the house was such that Nora could only see the blunt anonymous end of a triwheel from her window. Nick had her skimmer. But – Nora grasped at the notion – Nick had gone to the Everetts. Maybe Landsman Everett was bringing him back. Father openly admired the breeder, said he was a sound husbandsman and made a real contribution to society.

Nora sat very still, straining to hear Nick's voice or Landsman Everett's cheerful tenor. She heard only the subdued murmur of her mother's greeting, and then Father's curt baritone. When she caught the second deep male rumble, she ceased listening and turned back to the console. She did have exams to pass, and eavesdropping did not add to family unity.

Nora usually enjoyed computer-assisted drill. It put one on the mental alert. She enjoyed the challenge of completing the drill well within the allotted time. So, despite her concerns, she was soon caught up in her studies. She finished the final level of review with only one equation wrong. Her own fault. She'd skipped a step in her hurry to beat the computer's time. She could never understand why some kids said they were exhausted after a computer-assisted session. She always felt great.

'Nora!'

Her father's summons startled her. Had she missed his first call? He sounded angry. You never made Father call you twice.

'Coming!' Anxious not to irritate him, she ran down the ramp to the lower level, apologizing all the way. 'Sorry, Father, I was concentrating on CAI review . . .' and then she saw that the visitor was Counsellor Fremmeng. She muttered a nervous good evening. This was the time of year for Parent Consultations, and deficiencies were usually scheduled first. She couldn't have made that poor a showing . . . A glance at her father's livid face told her that this interview was not going the way George Fenn wanted it.

'Counsellor Fremmeng has informed me that *you* have achieved sufficient distinction in your schooling to warrant Academic Advancement.'

The savage way her father spat the words out and the disappointment on his face dried up any thought Nora had of exulting in her achievement. Hurt and bewildered, unaccountably rebuked in yet another effort to win his approval, Nora stared back at him. Even if she was a girl, surely he didn't hate her for getting Academic . . . In a sudden change of state, she realized why.

'Then Nick didn't?'

Her father turned from her coldly so that Counsellor Fremmeng had to confirm it. His eyes were almost sad in his long, jowled face. Didn't *he* take pride in her achievement? Didn't anyone? Crushed with disappointment, Nora pivoted slowly. When she met her mother's eyes, she saw in them something greater than mere approval. Something more like anticipation, entreaty.

'Your brother,' Father went on with such scathing bitterness that Nora shuddered, 'has been *tentatively* allowed two years of Applied Advancement. The wisdom of society has limited this to the Agricultural Institute with the recommendation that he study *animal husbandry*.' He turned back to face his daughter, eyes burning, huge frame rigid with emotion.

Serves him right, Nora thought, and quickly squelched such disrespect. He had been too certain that Nick would qualify for the university and become a Computer Master for the Fenn Complex. He'll just have to adjust. A Fenn is going on. Me.

'How . . .' and suddenly George Fenn erupted, seeking relief from his disappointment with violent pacing and exaggerated gestures of his big hands, 'how can a girl qualify when her brother, of the same parentage, raised in the same environment, given the same education at the same institution, receives only a tentative acceptance? Tentative! Why, Nicholas has twice the brains his sister has!'

'Not demonstrably, Landsman,' Counsellor Fremming remarked, flicking a cryptic glance at Nora. 'And certainly not the same intense application. Nick showed the most interest and diligence in biology and ecology. His term paper, an optional project on the mutation of angoran ovines, demonstrated an in-depth appreciation of genetic manipulation. Society encourages such –'

'But sheep!' Father interrupted him. 'Fenns are crop farmers.'

'A little diversity improves any operation,' Counsellor Fremming said with such uncharacteristic speciousness that Nora stared at him.

'My son may study sheep. Well then, what area of concentration has been opened to my . . . my daughter?'

Nora swallowed hard, wishing so much that Father would not look at her as if she'd been printed out by mistake. Then she realized that the Counsellor was looking at *her* to answer her father.

'I'd prefer to –'

'What area is she qualified to pursue?' Father cut her off peremptorily, again directing his question to the Counsellor.

The man cleared his throat as he flipped open his wrist recorder and made an adjustment. He studied the frame for a long moment. It gave Nora a chance to sort out her own thoughts. She really hadn't believed Nick this afternoon when he intimated he'd thwarted Father's plans. And she'd certainly never expected Academic!

The Counsellor tapped the side of the recorder thoughtfully, pursing his lips as he'd a habit of doing when he was trying to phrase a motivating reprimand to an underachiever.

'Nora is unusually astute in mathematics and symbolic

logic . . .' The Counsellor's eyes slid across her face, again that oblique warning. 'She has shown some marked skill in Computer Design, but in order to achieve Computer Technician . . .'

'Computer Tech – Could she actually make Technician status?' Father demanded sharply, and Nora could sense the change in him.

Counsellor Fremming coughed suddenly, covering his mouth politely. When he looked up again, Nora could almost swear he'd been covering a laugh, not a cough. His little eyes were very bright. None of the other kids believed her when she said that the Counsellor was actually human, with a sense of humour. Of course, a man in his position had to maintain dignity in front of the student body.

'I believe that is quite within her capability, Landsman,' Counsellor Fremming said in a rather strained voice.

'Didn't you say, Counsellor, that Nora qualified for unlimited Academic Advancement?' Mother asked quietly. She held Nora's eyes steadily for a moment before she turned with a little smile to her husband. 'So a Fenn *is* going on to university this generation, just as you hoped, George. Now, if you could see your way clear to diversify – And did you notice the premium angora fleece is bringing? You know how I've wanted young things to tend and lambs are so endearing. Why, I might even get Counsellor Fremmeng to recommend updating for me at the Institute. Then, George, you wouldn't need to spend all those credits for apprentices. The Fenns could work the Complex all by themselves. Just like the old days!'

'It's an encouraging thing for me to have such a contributing family unit in my Sector. A real pleasure,' Counsellor said, smiling at the older Fenns before he gave Nora a barely perceptible nod.

'Well, girl, so you'll study Computology at the university?' asked Father. His joviality was a little forced, and his eyes were still cold.

'I ought to take courses in Stability Phenomena, Feedback Control, more Disturbance Dynamics . . .'

'Listen to the child. You'd never think such terms would come so easily to a girl's lips, would you?' asked Father.

'Mathematics is scarcely a male prerogative, Landsman,'

said Counsellor Fremming, rising. 'It's the major tool of our present sane social structure. That and social dynamics. Nora's distinguished herself in social psychology, which is, as you know, the prerequisite for building the solid family relationships which constitute the foundation of our society.'

'Oh, she'll be a good mother in her time,' Father said, still with that horrible edge to his heartiness. His glance lingered on his wife.

'Undoubtedly,' the Counsellor agreed blandly. 'However, there's more to maintaining a sound family structure than maternity. As Nora has demonstrated. If you'll come to my office after your exams on Thursday, Nora, we'll discuss your programme at the university in depth, according to your potentials.' His slight emphasis on the pronoun went unnoticed by George Fenn. Then the Counsellor bowed formally to her parents, congratulated them again on the achievements of their children, their contribution to society, and left.

'So, girl,' her father said in a heavy tone, '*you'll* be the crop farmer in this generation.'

Nora faced him unable to perjure herself. With his pitiful honking about farming Fenns, he was like a goose, fattening for his own destruction. She felt pity for him because he couldn't see beyond his perch on these acres. But he was doing what he'd been set in this life to do, as the geese were making their contribution to society, too.

Unlimited Academic Advancement! She'd never anticipated that. But she could see that it was in great measure due to her father. Because he had considered her inferior to Nick, she'd worked doubly hard, trying to win his approval. She realized now that she'd never have it, Father being what he was. And being the person she was, she'd not leave him in discord. She'd help maintain family unity until Father came to accept Nick as a sheep-breeder, diversification on the Fenn acres, a Fenn daughter in the university. Mother would step in to help with crop farming and there'd be no decrease in contribution.

'I'll do all I can to help you, Father,' Nora said finally, realizing that her parents were waiting for her answer.

Then she caught her mother's shining eyes, saw in them the approval, the assurance she wanted. She knew she was the daughter her mother had wanted. *That* made her happy.

Notes on the writers and their stories

The time given for each story is an estimate of how long it should take for the story to be read aloud.

Dual Control by Elizabeth Walter

(15 minutes)

Elizabeth Walter is amongst the finest British writers to have specialised in the art of the ghost story. Her collections of uncanny tales include: *Showfall* (1965), *The Sin Eater* (1967), *Davy Jones' Tale* (1971), *Come and Get Me* (1973), and an American assembly of her work, *In the Mist, and Other Uncanny Encounters* (1979). 'Dual Control' is taken from *Dead Woman* (1975).

The character of Gisela, the ghost, is taken from an old story in which Giselle, a lovely young peasant woman, is betrayed by a prince and, as a result, goes mad and dies. After her death her spirit joins those of other betrayed young women in preying on young men who have lost their way.

Smoke by Ila Mehta

(12 minutes)

Ila Mehta was born in 1938 and is a Professor of Gujarati at St Xavier's College, Bombay. She has written for television and radio as well as writing short stories, novels and plays.

compounder man who looks after the complex of houses and gardens
Diwali Hindu festival
enhancing improving, increasing

incense fragrant material burned to honour a holy person
inconsequential unimportant
inexorably unrelentingly, with no let-up
intermittently from time to time
irrepressible uncontrollable
Krishna Hindu god
mundane dull, routine
obeisance bow or curtsey of respect
opaque not transparent
palpably so that it could be felt
permeating entering right into
russett reddish brown
scintillating sparkling, wittily entertaining
skeins tangled threads, webs

The Stolen Party by Liliana Heker

(10 minutes)

Liliana Heker was born in 1943 and comes from Argentina. During a time of censorship and repression, she remained in Argentina to fight for the writer's cause through her work. She writes in Spanish and is translated into English.

The Earth by Djuna Barnes

(10 minutes)

Djuna Barnes, an American who lived in Europe for many years, was born in 1892 and died in 1982. One of her books, called *Nightwood*, depicts a nightmare cosmopolitan world which is chiefly located in New York and Paris. It is an experimental novel in which the characters are tormented and torment each other. They are linked by an enigmatic doctor who is also a priest of the secret brotherhood of The City of Darkness. Her book of short stories is called *Smoke and Other Stories* and was published in 1983.

akimbo crossed
black bread bread made with rye flour
complacently in a self-satisfied way
evince express
flat beer central European beer made without fizz

impassible not able to feel emotion
keenness sharpness
knavery dishonest behaviour
mulled wine warm, spiced wine
ravine deep narrow gorge in mountains
sour cakes scone-type cakes made with sour milk
speculate form a theory
unperturbed calm
wick twisted threads of cotton in a candle or lamp

Looking for a Rain God by Bessie Head

(7 minutes)

Bessie Head was born in 1939 in Pietermaritzburg, South Africa, though she has lived in exile in Botswana since the 1960s. She has written about her home in *Serowe: Village of the Rain Wind* (1981). Her work often deals with the inner life of a black woman as she goes through different experiences. Many of her short stories are collected from the local people and are survivors from the ancient life of the people of Southern Africa.

anguish great suffering
charlatans people who pretend to have knowledge
drought long period of time without rain
incanters chanters of spells
inspanned harnessed to the plough
kgotla meeting place
proclamation official announcement
ritual murder killing or murder in the course of a religious service
talismans lucky charms

A Visit from the Footbinder by Emily Prager

(40 minutes)

Emily Prager is an American who grew up in Texas, the Far East and Greenwich Village. She studied anthropology and since then she has been contributing editor for *The National Lampoon* and for *Viva*. She writes short stories of surprising power, as well as humorous and critical articles.

aesthetic beautiful
artisan craftsman
askew not straight
belvedere raised summer-house with view
brocade fabric woven with patterns
calligraphic of decorative and artistic writing
catapult full-size weapon of war used to throw stones
cavorted danced
chastened corrected
cloying sickly sweet and heavy
commotion disturbance
conceptual abstract
concubine additional, secondary wife
courtesan high-class prostitute
decocted boiled so as to extract the essence
decoction liquid essence
deplete use up
ebbed died, faded
edifice building
effeminate delicate, girlish
elicit draw out
endeavour project
endure tolerate, put up with
ensued followed
fatigued tired
fraught with loaded with
frolicking skipping and dancing
frugal careful with money
geomancer magician in touch with earth forces
haggling bargaining
haughtily proudly
immodest not correct, impudent
imperious domineering
inaugural opening
incense fragrant material burned to honour a holy person
indubitable certain
ingratiate himself make himself pleasing
jasmine white flower with very strong perfume
lacquer coloured varnish
lacquered varnished with colour
legacy inheritance

lotus type of waterlily
malleable adapted, flexible
meditated studied
mêlée scuffle
mesmerized hypnotized
Mongol hordes conquering people who came from the steppes of Asia
mongoose small Indian animal which can kill poisonous snakes
netherworld world after death
nonchalantly casually
opulent rich and full
orchid fantastic and brilliant flower
overwrought tense, stressed
pavilions light ornamental buildings
perceived saw
permeated entered right into
prefecture government district
propitiate make favourable
propitious favourable
pungent strong and aromatic
python snake which crushes its victims
queasy slightly sick
quizzically mockingly
regale treat, feast
Resignation unhappy acceptance
saffron yellow
scepticism doubt
sedan chair covered chair used to carry somone
sentiments feelings
sickle curved blade
sluffed cast off
stoically indifferent to pleasure and pain
Taoist of Taoism (a Chinese religion)
travesty mockery
ubiquitous found everywhere
unerring accurate
Venerable Highly Honoured (title of deep respect)
wanton self-indulgent, sensual
zither stringed instrument held on the lap

The Kiss by Angela Carter

(7 minutes)

Angela Carter was born in 1940, in Sussex, and died in 1992. She read English at Bristol University, lived in Japan and taught Creative Writing at Sheffield University, at Brown University, Rhode Island, USA, and Adelaide University, Australia. Her novels and short stories are highly regarded, and she won several major prizes for her writing.

cesspits pits for collecting dirty water and sewage
cholera an infectious, often fatal disease
dysentery a disease affecting the intestines
ensorcellate bewitch
exoticism attractive strangeness
fabulous legendary
foetid stinking
garnets deep red jewels
imminent fast approaching
kernels inner seeds or nuts
kohl fine black powder
lapis lazuli vivid blue semi-precious stone
mausoleums magnificent tombs
ochre pale brownish-yellow
pistachio nuts with greenish edible kernel
Scheherezade girl who marries a Sultan who is so convinced that all women are faithless he executes his new brides the morning after the wedding; Scheherezade begins to tell him a story which does not reach its end by the time she is supposed to be executed, so the Sultan keeps her alive to hear the end of the story; Scheherezade manages to keep this going for 1001 nights; then the Sultan changes his mind and decides he loves her
scourge instrument of divine punishment
Tamburlaine (1336–1405) Mongol conqueror of India, Russia, Persia and Central Asia
terracotta brownish-red colour
veridian (normally spelled viridian) bluish-green
welch fail to pay

To Hell with Dying by Alice Walker
(12 minutes)

Alice Walker was born in 1944 in Eatonton, Georgia, USA. Her family were sharecroppers (tenant farmers) and her writing is about personal and family relationships. She is particularly concerned with the way that black women deal with sexism and racism, which she describes in a precise and unsentimental manner. She has been active in the civil rights movement and in teaching Black Studies. Her writing includes poetry, short story and novel, including the widely acclaimed *The Color Purple*.

acute sharp
coherent understandable
contemptuous scornful
crossover passing from life to death
dallying delaying
devastating overwhelmingly beautiful
diabetic person with disease which prevents the body using sugar and starch normally
dilapidated run-down
dissertation long essay
doctorate high academic degree
expiring dying
impenetrable impossible to get into
implacable inexorable, unstoppable
keeling over falling over
kick the bucket die
liniment ointment for rubbing on muscles
melancholy gloomy
rehabilitation restoration
rickety unstable
rite solemn ceremony
squall loud yell

Here We Are by Dorothy Parker
(12 minutes)

Dorothy Parker was born in 1893 in New Jersey, USA; she lived mostly in New York, and died in 1967. She was noted for her biting wit, and this is echoed in her writing, which usually comments on departing or departed love. She hated sentimentality and stupidity, and was instrumental in developing the modern taste for refined and clever humour. She worked for *Vogue*, *Vanity Fair* and *The New Yorker* and wrote poetry as well as short stories.

dispensed given out
novelty newness
phenomena wonders
plush velvety fabric
Pullman especially comfortable railway carriage
raptly absorbedly
rendering making
sporadic occasional

Two Hanged Women by Henry Handel Richardson
(6 minutes)

Henry Handel Richardson was the 'pen name' of Ethel Florence Richardson. Her English parents emigrated to Australia and she was born in 1870. At seventeen she went to Leipzig in Germany to study piano for three years. Later she married a Professor of German at London University and spent much of her life in England, though she travelled a lot. Her writing often has musical themes. She wrote full-length novels as well as short stories. She died in 1946.

amatory loving
flaxen blonde
cock of the eye look
contemptuous scornful
ebbing dying away
esplanade public walkway by the sea
fervour passion
Harris tweeds rough woollen cloth hand-woven in the Outer Hebrides
pegged walked vigorously
putrid rotten
reek smell strongly
salvo sudden sound (as of a burst of gunfire)
skittish playful

slothfully lazily
sole only
sombre dark and gloomy
tranquil calm
unyielding not giving way
vehemence violence

The Lottery by Marjorie Barnard
(7 minutes)

Marjorie Barnard was a novelist, children's writer, historian and biographer. She was born in 1897 in Sydney, Australia, and lived mainly in New South Wales until her death in 1987. In the late 1930s she became a pacifist. She wrote in collaboration with other writers between the 1920s and the 1950s. Her outstanding novel *Tomorrow and Tomorrow and Tomorrow* (1947) was awarded the Patrick White prize only in 1983. Her collection of short stories, *The Persimmon Tree,* was published in 1943.

Anzac Day the official holiday to remember the soldiers of Second World War in Australia and New Zealand
chromium pipes of the pneumatic system in the past customers in a shop handed their money to the shop assistant, who placed it in a container which was taken to a central cashier through air tubes; the cashier dealt with the money and the change and returned it to the shop assistant in the same way
derisive mocking
flaccid limp
idyllic picturesque and perfect
jaunty cheerful
namby-pamby soft
nonchalantly carelessly
perversity deliberate awkwardness
serrating cutting into a jagged shape
spasm sudden contraction of muscles
stature size and status
trousseau bride's outfit
truncated cut off
wag cheerful joker

Daughter by Anne McCaffrey

(38 minutes)

Anne McCaffrey is one of the world's leading science-fiction writers. She has won both the Hugo and the Nebula awards for fiction and is the creator of the Dragon series. She was brought up in the United States and now lives in Ireland. She was educated at Radcliffe College, Massachusetts, USA, and has a degree in Slavonic Languages and Literature.

altercations quarrels
amiably in a friendly way
angoran ovines long-haired sheep
antiquated old-fashioned
aptitudes abilities
arbitrary random
arbour shady retreat
aspirations hopes
astute intelligent
atavist person who is extremely old-fashioned
berate tell off
biddable obedient
cantankerous bad-tempered
cerebral intellectual
change state change emotions
clarion like a clear trumpet
coercion force
colony ship space ship which takes people to settle a new planet
complied with followed
constitutional right right given by the state
contributory helping
credentials qualifications
creditable bringing honour
cull take out and destroy the useless or unsuitable
curt abrupt
deficiency lacks
delectation delight
dictum formal saying
diligence hard work
disconcertingly disturbingly
disconsolately sadly

disparaged thought nothing of
diversify introduce variety
electives options
engrossing fascinating
ergot diseased corn
evaluation assessment
exigencies demands
filaments strands
flippancy lack of seriousness
forbearance patience
gleaners people who followed the corn reapers to pick up what they left
gourmet expert on eating
harangued loudly criticized
heralded announced
heritage birthright
impartial fair
incredulously in disbelief
ineradicably permanently
inherent natural, inborn
intangible difficult to touch or measure
intemperate hot-headed and unrestrained
interceded pleaded on someone else's behalf
keep unity stay in agreement
loquacity talkativeness
multipentangle many-sided building
muted soft, quiet
nauseating sickening
parameters limits
peremptorily in a way which allowed no refusal
plaint complaint
pragmatist practical person
quibble argue about details, especially words
reamed told off
replenished refilled
resolutely with determination
reverberation echo
sanctuary protection
Saturnalia Roman mid-winter festival
scrupulously extremely carefully
sluice gate gate that holds back water in an irrigation system

speciousness apparent (but not actual) correctness
static (here) hassle, interference
subsistence minimum
summation summing up
tacit silent
tangent side issue
tentatively provisionally
thwarting frustrating
tirades storms of words
tracts strips of land
trilevel habitation house on three levels
turned to ergot became diseased
vagrant loose
whimsy fancy
winnow separate the grain from the loose plant-material (old farming term)
Winter Solstice mid-winter festival

Acknowledgements

The author and publisher would like to thank the following for their kind permission to reproduce stories in this book:

'Dual Control' reproduced by kind permission of the author, © Elizabeth Walter 1975, and first published in *Dead Woman and Other Haunting Experiences*, Collins Harvill 1975; 'Smoke' by Ila Mehta first appeared in *Truth Tales: Stories by Indian Women*, originally published by Kali for Women, A-36 Gulmohar Park, New Delhi 110 049, India (1986) and first published in Great Britain by The Women's Press Ltd; 'The Stolen Party' by Liliana Heker, reproduced by permission of Vardey & Brunton Associates, copyright © 1982 by Liliana Heker, translation copyright © 1985 by Alberto Manguel; 'The Earth' by Djuna Barnes reproduced by permission of the Estate of Djuna Barnes, Virago Press Ltd and Sun and Moon Press, California; 'Looking for a Rain God' from *The Collector of Treasures* by Bessie Head, published by Heinemann International Literature and Textbooks and reproduced with their permission; 'A Visit from the Footbinder' from *A Visit from the Footbinder and Other Stories* by Emily Prager, published by Chatto & Windus, reproduced by permission of Random Century Group; 'The Kiss' from *Black Venus* by Angela Carter, published by Chatto & Windus, reproduced by permission of the Estate of the author and Random Century Group; 'To Hell with Dying' by Alice Walker from *In Love and Trouble*, published by The Women's Press Ltd 1984, reproduced by permission of David Higham Associates; 'Here We Are' by Dorothy Parker, reproduced by permission of Gerald Duckworth & Co Ltd; 'Two Hanged Women' from *The Adventures of Cuffy Mahony* by Henry Handel Richardson, reproduced by permission of Collins / Angus & Robertson Publishers; 'The Lottery' by Marjorie Barnard, reproduced with permission of Curtis Brown Ltd, London, copyright © Marjorie Barnard 1943; 'Daughter' by Anne McCaffrey, copyright © Anne McCaffrey 1971, extracted from *Get Off the Unicorn*, published by Transworld Publishers Ltd, all rights reserved.

Every effort has been made to reach all the copyright holders; the publishers would be glad to hear from anyone whose rights have been unknowingly infringed.

We would also like to thank Liliana Heker for allowing us to use 'The Stolen Party' as the title for this collection.